And the two runaways opened the massive oak door of the sexton's house, climbed up and up and up endless winding stairs, higher and higher, and finally came at the very top to a green door with a polished brass handle...

"Come in, come in!" a friendly voice called in answer to Anemone's knock. "Come in, unless you're a man. Just press the latch and the door will open."

Anemone obeyed. She stepped into a narrow hallway, and from there into the strangest imaginable room...

"This book has everything: gargoyles, a girl who runs away to join the circus, wise animals and a magic puppet show, an evil tyrant and a happy ending. I'm glad to see it's finally being issued in paperback."

—Lisa Goldstein, American Book
Award-winning author of
The Dream Years

THE WICKED ENCHANTMENT

MARGOT BENARY-ISBERT

ACE FANTASY BOOKS
NEW YORK

Translated from the German by
Richard and Clara Winston.

This Ace Fantasy Book
contains the complete text of
the original hardcover edition. It has been
completely reset in a typeface
designed for easy reading, and
was printed from new film.

THE WICKED ENCHANTMENT

An Ace Fantasy Book/published by arrangement with
Harcourt Brace Jovanovich, Inc.

PRINTING HISTORY
Harcourt, Brace & World edition published 1955
Ace Fantasy edition/March 1986

ISBN: 0-441-88669-8

Ace Fantasy Books are published by The Berkley Publishing Group,
200 Madison Avenue, New York, New York 10016.
PRINTED IN THE UNITED STATES OF AMERICA

CONTENTS

THE WICKED ENCHANTMENT

OUR OLD TOWN lies right in the middle of Germany, on the road between Nowhere and Somewhere. It is surrounded by green hills, and through it run gaily the arms of the swift little river which turn the wheels of our mills. To a traveler passing through, our town probably doesn't look very different from a hundred other medieval German towns. It has its crooked streets and a marketplace, several churches, a few cloisters, and a proud town hall with a beautiful old fountain in front of it. The name of our town is Vogelsang, which means Birdsong. It has that pretty name because for hundreds of years the singing birds have come in great flocks to make their nests in our orchards and have sung more sweetly than anywhere else.

In one way, though, our town is rather distinctive. It has a famous ancient gothic cathedral which sits high on a hill, towering above the net of narrow streets. We are

1

proud of our cathedral. On the other hand we know that it is the reason why odd and spooky things are apt to happen in Vogelsang. But since we are used to such goings on we don't make much of a fuss about them as long as they don't get out of hand.

You see, the masons and architects of the olden times who built those cathedrals used to put all kinds of uncanny and sometimes frightening figures on the roofs and turrets. There are waterspouts and gargoyles and such, perched high up and looking down on the city with grinning, horrible faces. In Vogelsang, some of them do not always behave as quietly as figures of stone should. But that is not all. *Beneath* our cathedral, in the deep vaults and crypts, are many caskets with elaborately carved lids, tombs in which members of the nobility and of patrician families sleep or at least are supposed to sleep peacefully until doomsday. But some of them don't, that's just the trouble, and then it may happen that they carry on as wickedly as the gargoyles outside. One of them has a deplorably bad reputation among the spooks of Vogelsang. I dimly remember my grandfather telling me about him and calling him the Wicked Owl, but I did not hear of him again until . . . That is what I am going to tell you about in this book.

There is a carved image of this man on the great slab of limestone that is the lid of his coffin. He lies there with armor and sword; at his head is his heraldic bird, a big stone owl; at his feet his name, the letters worn by age, *Earl Owl of Owlhall*. For years and years nobody had gone down into this vault where the Wicked Owl lies buried. As a matter of fact, the entrance to this vault had been forgotten and so had the Wicked Owl.

I might as well admit that people in neighboring towns, those Nowhere-ers and Somewhere-ers, for example, say we are all a little touched. "The crazy Vogelsangers" they call us. But that doesn't bother us a bit. We know what we know, and of course we wouldn't for the world be anything *but* Vogelsangers, whatever they may think about us. We do not complain about our spooks, as there is seldom any reason to complain. Most of them are as nice and respectable as we could wish, and they don't scare us in the least when we meet up with them—say while sitting on a bench of old Petersberg cemetery or coming home a little late from The Merry Finch. A perfectly natural thing to happen, we think, and there's no sense trying to explain it away by all sorts of farfetched theories.

What I want to tell you about, however, is one occurrence that did not turn out as peacefully as most of our experience with ghosts, and which resulted in the Great Vogelsang Rebellion, or, as some chronicles call it, the Battle of the Easter Eggs.

But I'd better begin at the beginning.

Flight

THE CLOCKS OF the many towers of our town were just chiming six when Anemone and her silvery-gray dog Winnie-the-Pooh, named after Anemone's favorite book, finished their climb up the hundred steps of Cathedral Hill and stopped to catch their breath.

"So here we are," the girl said to the dog, and Winnie looked up at her with clever black-cherry eyes, wagging her stub of a tail in agreement. She was a dog of rare and precious blood, a Kerry-blue terrier from England. But she was remarkable in another respect, too, because she understood, and usually agreed with, every word her young mistress said.

"So here we are," Anemone repeated. "And what next?" But even clever Winnie had no answer to that.

It was a cold, damp evening in March. The sun, a blood-red ball, was just setting behind Swedish Fort Hill. From the height on which the cathedral stood you could

5

see down to the wide square where booths were being set up for the Easter Fair. Hammers were thumping and saws grating and men shouting as they put up the little wooden booths and worked away at the huge circus tent.

"We can't possibly go back home," Anemone said. "Or do you think we can?"

Winnie growled, and it was perfectly plain to her mistress that she was saying, "Never again."

"No, this was the last straw," Anemone went on. "I'd sooner freeze in the cold March wind than bear it any longer."

The two runaways stood thoughtfully in the cold, feeling pretty low in spirit.

It was almost two years since Anemone's mother had died. Although they still missed her terribly, father and daughter had managed quite well by themselves. Mr. Florus was a nursery gardener, as all his forefathers had been. He raised rare and beautiful flowers in his gardens and greenhouses, and gathered precious seed which was in great demand all over the countryside. Anemone looked after the house and the animals of which her mother had been so fond. There was the trio of fleecy milk-sheep. There was the proud rooster with his six hens, the hedgehog family that lived under the beechwood hedge, the handsome salamanders, the red-bellied newts in the cool stone caves by the little pond, and the useful lizards, frogs and toads which kept Mr. Florus's flowerbeds free from harmful insects. Not to be forgotten was the multitude of birds that lived in the trees and shrubs of the garden, bathing in the bird-bath among the wild roses in the summertime, and in the winter, those that stayed, taking their feed from Anemone's hand.

All these creatures had lived happily with the Florus family from time immemorial until the day last fall when a strange woman, called Ilsebill, had entered the old Florus house and brought her son Erwin with her. On a stormy, rainy evening there had been a knock at the door, Mr. Florus had opened it, and had faced a woman in a gray dress and coat, her boy clinging shivering to her skirts. In a plaintive voice she had asked for shelter and a job, asserting that she was a homeless, poor, hard-working widow, and didn't Mr. Florus need a house-keeper?

Anemone couldn't see the slightest reason why they should need a housekeeper. But her father was too good-hearted to turn the woman and her son out into the cold night again. And so the two of them stayed.

Hardworking she was, Anemone had to give her credit for that. All day long she rushed around the house with broom and dustcloth, mop, water pail and cleaning rags. She was a marvelous cook, too, and how she disposed of the dishes after each meal so quickly and efficiently was more than Anemone could understand. She herself had run the household as a kind of sideline, since she had to go to school every day from eight to one o'clock and twice a week for two more hours in the afternoon. The main thing, she and her father had always felt, was to keep cozy and cheerful. Dishwashing was put off until not a cup or plate was left in the closet. "Dust-mice under the beds and sunlight in your heart" was one of their favorite sayings. And how comfortable they had been sitting at the fireplace in the evening. Winnie slept on the rug, while they read happily by the hour and then told each other what they had been reading.

But since that woman with her cleaning craze had come along, everything had changed.

Perhaps Mr. Florus liked the way his chest of drawers was now always filled with neatly darned socks and freshly

ironed shirts. Perhaps he liked being served new appe-
tizing dishes every day, especially a kind of dumpling
he declared out of this world, when all Anemone used
to cook was spinach with eggs and rice pudding. After
all she was only eleven years old. Anyhow, Ilsebill had
gradually wormed her way into Mr. Florus's favor and
he seemed to be fairly content with the new regime.

On top of it all Ilsebill had a way of making her son
Erwin appear like a little angel. Almost every day she
told Mr. Florus that she would gladly make Anemone
into a well-behaved child just like her son, if only she
could have a free hand with the girl.

Well-behaved child indeed! A worse rascal than Erwin
could hardly be imagined. And the idea of being "taken
in hand" by Ilsebill gave Anemone the shivers. She and
Winnie were not deceived for a minute by her false-faced
friendliness. Nobody had ever considered Anemone a
problem child. She had been allowed to do whatever
gave her pleasure, and so far she had never been a bother
to anyone.

Anemone was not afraid for herself, but every day
she was grieved and horrified by the way the housekeeper
and her son treated all the good animal-friends around
the house and garden. If Erwin pulled out a prized flower,
he would shamelessly say that Little Pearl, the lamb, had
nipped it. If he had trampled a flowerbed, his mother
would lay the blame on the hens. Then she said they did
not lay eggs anyway—those nasty birds were only eating
their heads off, no use to keep them any longer. And one
after another they found a sad end in her soup pot.
Anemone wept bitter tears over the fate of her feathered
friends, and would not eat a bite of chicken, no matter
how temptingly Ilsebill served it.

Then there was the event with the lizard. Erwin had

carelessly left the doors open and one of the graceful little things had found its way into Ilsebill's bedroom. She raised the roof, shrieking bloody murder over the "disgusting vermin." She took on as if the harmless lizard were at least a Gila monster. And at supper that day she came out with a whole series of stories about people who had been bitten and poisoned by such creatures. If you asked her, she said, those lizards, toads and newts had infested the garden were in the same class as vipers.

Anemone contradicted her violently. Frogs didn't snap, and lizards didn't bite she said, and even if they did they weren't poisonous. But good-natured Mr. Florus, who wanted everybody to be happy, agreed to do what he could to clean out these harmless beasts, because his housekeeper was so frightened of them. He had to admit to Anemone that he considered all this talk about poisoning just a kind of supersitition. But for the sake of harmony in the house, he said, a person had to make compromises—and Ilsebill could certainly make wonderful dumplings.

Triumphant with her victory over the "vermin" Ilsebill at last started a campaign for getting rid of Winnie. In the meantime the poor dog was teased and tormented by Erwin, and if she let out a yip or tried to defend herself, Ilsebill pointed this out as another example of how mean and vicious she was. Such a dog, she said, should be kept on a chain or given to the dogcatcher; otherwise she was sure to hurt somebody one of these days. Before long, Mr. Florus, hearing day in and day out his housekeeper's complaints, began to treat poor Winnie with marked coldness—he who had been so fond of the little dog who had been his dead wife's pet. Anemone was very sorry about all this. In fact, she began to doubt whether her father loved her as much as he used to. They disagreed about almost everything nowadays—and only a short while ago they had been the best of friends.

If Anemone had been a timid and complacent little girl, perhaps nothing would have happened for a while. But she had a mind of her own, and she simply couldn't keep her mouth shut when she caught Erwin at one of his nasty tricks. When he smashed up birds' nests, threw stones at the lizards and fished the minnows out of the pond only to see them die miserably on the grass, she did not hold back with her opinion, and maybe the names she called the wretched boy were not always very mild or polite. She had learned from her mother that there is nothing so slow as killing defenseless creatures.

So it was not surprising that she and Ilsebill and Erwin could not get along together. And today the terrible end had come. Anemone had taken Winnie on the leash and left her father's house because she had learned that even from her beloved Papa she could not expect justice any longer.

"No, Winnie," she said, while the rough March wind whistled about her ears, "we won't go back as long as THEY are in the house. For this is tyranny, and we are all against it, aren't we? All Papa cares about is Ilsebill's dumplings. There's not help for it, we must manage by ourselves. But first we'd better see where we are going to sleep tonight."

That was easier said than done.

Down below lay the town in the twilight mist. The crescent moon, wrapped in clouds, and the dim light of street lanterns did little to illuminate the buildings across the broad square. But Anemone knew some of them so well that she could recognize them by their outlines. There was the crooked little house where Uncle Eusebius lived like a hermit, surrounded by innumerable books, strange masks and weapons from foreign lands, musical instruments of all kinds, and yellowed papers. Uncle Eusebius was considered one of the town's most distinguished scholars and experts in ornithology. Some years ago he had gone on a trip around the world, but after this regrettable mistake he had settled down in his hometown again. He held the title of Art-and-Church Councilor of Vogelsang and had been entrusted with the honorable task of collecting the songs of all the different kinds of birds living in and passing through Vogelsang for the great Bird Archives of the town. And of course he was a prominent member of the Bird Club.

Anemone had visited Uncle Eusebius with her father several times, and had greatly enjoyed these visits. Still, she didn't fancy the idea of asking him to put her up for the night. The queer masks and fetishes in his rooms were interesting enough to look at by daylight, but she did not know whether she would like to sleep under the penetrating gaze of their mother-of-pearl eyes.

Not far away, in the street known as Crooked Alley, lived another uncle, Privy Councilor and Doctor of Philosophy Rafael Trippstrill and his kindly wife Lena. She would certainly have been glad to take in a motherless and homeless little girl. And so would Aunt Tina, who was married to Town Architect Agamemnon Winkelriss. Both of these ladies had been devoted to Anemone's mother, and Anemone could be sure of a warm welcome in either house.

But as Anemone knew only too well, the Trippstrills and Winkelrisses had fallen on hard times lately, and she wouldn't want to be a burden.

Until recently Trippstrill had been curator of the art collections and the curio cabinet of Vogelsang, and Winkelriss had been in charge of the repairs constantly going on upon the ancient, historic buildings of the town. For many years they had held these offices and everybody had been more than satisfied with them. But last fall a new mayor had taken over in the city hall, and things had started going wrong. This new man was a stranger; nobody knew exactly how he had come to hold office. Very soon he had started to change everything in the administration of the town, and for Anemone's learned uncles he had another commission about every week, one of them being the cleaning and restoration of a group of stone statues in some outside niches of the cathedral. These statues represented the Wise and Foolish Virgins from the Bible, and in the course of centuries the tooth of time had done quite a bit of gnawing away at them.

The three experts, Trippstrill, Winkelriss and Eusebius, had their doubts about the advisability of tampering with the statues. But the mayor insisted, and so at great trouble and expense the stone maidens were removed from their places and transferred to an unused vestry of the cathedral, where they were with all possible care restored and refurbished. By January, the Wise and Foolish Virgins looked as good as the day they were carved, and the mayor made an official statement about the boost this project would give to Vogelsang's tourist trade. A parade was arranged for the day they were to be replaced in their niches.

Everyone gathered on Cathedral Hill for the ceremony. The mayor appeared in gown and golden chain, the aldermen in their black sallowtail Sunday coats. A crowd of spectators had assembled.

And then—imagine the alarm and the shock! It turned out that one of the Foolish Virgins was missing! They counted backward and forward, but that did not alter the situation: there were only four Foolish Virgins instead of five.

What a disgrace for Vogelsang that one of the niches should remain empty! That would be grist to the mills of the neighboring towns, who were always lying in wait for a new reason to sneer. And as though that were not enough, one of the waterspouts was missing, too. Since time immemorial that gargoyle had crouched above the head of the Foolish Virgin and spewed the rain water down on the pavement. It had been the pride and joy of Vogelsang, for no other cathedral in the country had one so downright hideous. Even for a gothic waterspout this one had been remarkably ugly, and from a scientific point of view this is the highest praise for a gargoyle.

So that was the situation—a missing Virgin and a missing waterspout. Trippstrill, Winkelriss and Eusebius were in a nasty fix indeed. And the mayor was not inclined to make it easier for them. Quite the contrary. He was beside himself with rage, and seemed to have forgotten that it had been he who had started the whole business. He called the three officials to the town hall and in the presence of the whole Board of Aldermen he gave them a severe dressing-down.

"You are relieved of your duties until the missing Virgin and the precious gargoyle are back in their places," he stormed. "I have no use for officials I cannot rely on. I'll give you time until after Easter. If they are not back by then, you will find yourselves facing a court of law."

Of course there was much grumbling among the townsfolk about the way the mayor was treating those honorable and popular men. But the sympathy of the population did not help them a bit. They had lost their positions, and before long they would have to face a trial.

That was what Anemone had picked up from the talk of grown-up people. She was an inquisitive kind of girl, and she loved to listen to all kinds of gossip whenever

she had a chance to do so. And there certainly was talk
enough going on in Vogelsang since this new mayor had
taken over. Anemone did not understand it all, of course,
but she felt thrilled and mystified by it and she wanted
to hear a lot more about these strange goings on.

But the immediate question now was to decide where
she and her dog were going to spend the night. She
thought hard about it, and all of a sudden she clapped
her hands. Why, here on Cathedral Hill, in the attic rooms
of the old sexton's house where Aunt Gundula lived,
they would find the best shelter they could wish for.

"She will put us up, Winnie," Anemone cried happily.
"Aunt Gundula was one of Mama's three best friends.
She won't tell on us, with her we are safe, absolutely!"

And the two runaways opened the massive oak door
of the sexton's house, climbed up and up and up endless
winding stairs, higher and higher, and finally came at
the very top to a green door with a polished brass handle
and a white enamel nameplate on which was written in
beautiful curlicue letters:

Gundula Immofila
Confectioner and Painter

Aunt Gundula

"COME IN, COME in!" a friendly voice called in answer to Anemone's knock. "Come in unless you're a man. Just press the latch and the door will open."

Anemone obeyed. She stepped into a narrow hallway, and from there into the strangest imaginable room. To the two freezing fugitives it felt as though they had come out of the dampness and cold of the raw March evening into the mild and lovely air of a garden in summertime. Growing plants stretched out their tendrils along the walls and down from the top of many bookcases, and among this greenhouse freshness nodded flowers of many shapes and colors. Large bowls held blossoming bulbs of snowdrop, crocus and narcissus, and all around the flowers buzzed golden-brown bees. The floor was covered from wall to wall with a moss-green rug, embroidered with a thousand tiny flower buds. On a soft cushion, busily cleaning herself, sat a stately gray cat, and on a polished brass rod a vivid parrot swung back and forth, beating

its wings violently and croaking, "Come in unless you're
a man, come in unless you're a man."

"Be still, Lora!" a voice fluted from the window. And
there she herself sat in a flowered dressing gown, in front
of a table littered with paints, bowls of water and little
platters for mixing colors: Aunt Gundula. She had a
paintbrush behind each ear, and her black hair was hanging in unruly curls. Her eyes, blue as a spring sky, smiled
at Anemone. She was sitting in an easy chair by the
window, from which she could overlook Cathedral Square
far below, and the whole of the Old Town. Round about
her, on narrow shelves along the wall, stood figurines of
animals and plants. There were animals of leather, glass,
clay, fiber and wood; plants made of wire and tinfoil,
scraps of cloth, colored wooden beads and buttons. Gundula Immofila's clever hands had fashioned all these things
for the delight of the children of Vogelsang. But the most
beautiful object in this room was the chair in which she
sat. It was deep, soft and comfortable, brocaded all over
with the gayest flowers, so natural and so fresh that you
were tempted to try to pick them. And then there were
books, so many of them that it made Anemone's eyes
gleam.

"So there you are, Anemone," Aunt Gundula said, as
though she had been expecting this visit. "Welcome, and
welcome to you, too, Winnie, daughter of the famous
Skilligaly. Nice of you to come."

"May we stay awhile?" Anemone asked.

"Of course. There is room enough in my big bed for
a whole family, and Winnie can sleep with Minette-the-
Cat. All day long I have felt a twitch in my left elbow,
and that always means company is coming."

"How handy," Anemone said, and sat down in another
easy chair opposite the table. "That way you can always
bake a cake in advance."

Gundula went quietly on with her painting, only glancing up now and then to throw a look at Anemone.

"Run away, hm?" she said at last. "Well, well. My birds have been telling me all sorts of things lately. The poor hens put in the soup pot over at somebody's house, and poison set out for the hedgehogs who used to live their modest lives in the beechwood hedge. A fine bag of tricks. And now even you are being driven out. Don't tell me that Ilsebill has already become your stepmother?"

"Ilsebill my stepmother?" Anemone cried out, thoroughly shocked. As a matter of fact she had let herself dream a little about a new mother lately, since a schoolmate of hers had got such a nice one. But to think of Ilsebill as that—Heaven forbid!

"No!" she said. "Papa would never think of anything so horrible. That is not why we went away. It is, it was . . . because something—well, something happened."

"Tell me about it," Gundula said.

"You see, it was this way. Erwin started to push a darning needle through Winnie's ear—isn't that the limit? Naturally Winnie snapped at him—any dog would have done that."

"Probably," Gundula agreed.

"And then I came along, hearing Winnie howl. And naturally I took the needle away from Erwin and stuck it in the lobe of *his* ear."

"Oh! Aha!" Gundula said.

"That's tit for tat, isn't it? And I told him what I thought of him, which was perhaps not exactly flattering. He ran away bawling to his mama and she started screaming, too, as though I had killed him, when it was only the darning needle he was going to stick through Winnie's ear, the mean old thing. And then off they ran to Papa together."

"And then?" Gundula asked interestedly, not looking half as indignant as most grownups would have. That was one of her nice features, she really wasn't so very grown-up after all, even though there were a few gray strands in her black hair. "I hope your father gave Erwin a good tanning on the seat of his pants," she said.

"That's what everybody would expect," Anemone said. "But what really happened was that Papa go mad at Winnie and me, and weren't we absolutely innocent? Of course Erwin's ear was bleeding a bit, but I was not allowed to say one single word to explain it all. Now would you call that fair? I was to go to my room, Papa said, and stay there for the rest of the day without any supper. I didn't mind the supper because I couldn't have eaten anyway, but poor Winnie was to be chained up to the old doghouse under the porch—Winnie who has been running free all her life and only snapped at Erwin because he tormented her. You know what I call that, Aunt Gundula? That's tyranny, and Winnie and I are all against it, aren't we, Winnie darling?"

"Oh, so you are against tyranny, are you," Aunt Gundula said rather thoughtfully.

"We are, absolutely. And on top of it all Papa allowed Ilsebill to punish me."

"And did she?"

"Didn't she! She said I was to apologize to Erwin and give him a kiss, think of that. Of course I didn't do it. And then she told me to write twenty times in my notebook: A gentle disposition must be every woman's ambition."

"Well, well. I had not the impression so far that *hers* is so very gentle."

Anemone considered that for a moment. "It's rather confusing," she said then. "Sometimes it is, and sometimes it isn't. When Papa is around she can be very gentle indeed, and her voice can be as sweet as sugar, and she blinks her eyes in the funniest way and says what a pity it is that I am so horrid to Erwin, and shouldn't Papa be a little stricter with me?"

"But, Anemone," Aunt Gundula exclaimed, "you don't mean to tell me your clever father is deceived by that sort of thing."

"Dumplings," Anemone said dolefully. "She makes wonderful dumplings, and Papa is crazy about dumplings. If I tried to complain about her, he would just think I was jealous. It's no use. He said he didn't want to see me for the rest of the day, and now he'll never see me again."

"Dear, dear," Aunt Gundula said, and she popped a paintbrush into her mouth to point its end. "Well, we'll sleep on the matter and talk about it some more tomorrow. School, for example—we have to decide what to do about that."

"But, Aunt Gundula, the Easter holidays start day after tomorrow."

"How convenient. And now I'll get out that cake I baked earlier. On account of my elbow, you know. Winnie can drink from Minette's milk bowl and share the cushion."

Anemone beckoned to the dog. Somewhat charily, Winnie approached the milk bowl, stiff-legged and with the hair of her neck standing on end. She did not quite trust the big gray cat. But Minette-the-Cat graciously permitted her visitor to lap up the milk, and she even moved aside slightly to make room on the cushion. Winnie's eyes widened as she saw, sleeping peacefully between Minette's velvety paws, a delicate little white mouse.

"Why, yes," Gundula said as Anemone, too, looked astonished. "At least here we still have peace." Then she went out to the kitchen and brought back a large slice of fresh cake for Anemone, who suddenly realized how hungry she was. "Nobody can bake as good cakes as you," she said, munching delightedly.

"Really? Not even Ilsebill? Well, there are eggs in my cakes, because I don't put my chickens into the soup pot."

"But I thought the mayor has bought up all the eggs in town?"

"So he has," Gundula nodded smugly. "But not mine. And farm women from the whole countryside bring me a few eggs every market day, hidden under the lettuce and the last of the winter cabbage that they are bringing to sell. They know I need an extra supply right now to paint for Easter eggs—my own three hens can't possibly lay enough. The farm women know all the secret paths through the mountains and the woods. They love to fool fat old Schlummermutz, the Chief Constable, and smuggle their eggs into town."

"Tell me some more," Anemone begged. "Nobody can tell fables and fairy tales like you."

"Fables and fairy tales indeed," Gundula said tartly. "It's nothing more nor less than the truth. I know everything that goes on in town and country—my birds bring me the news. Partly because we're old friends, but partly because they all want to get into the big book I'm preparing on all the birds in the area. There will be pictures of each one in natural colors—the tiny common wren and his golden-crested cousin, the titmice and finches, the blackbirds and thrushes, nightingale and lark, and of course the beautiful pigeons who are my closest neighbors, since they live right here in the gables of this house and in the cathedral towers. They all come and sit for me so that I can paint every little feather. You can't imagine how proud they are to see themselves in paint. And while they sit they tell me tales. They come from everywhere, and there's little that gets by them."

Gundula took out a large portfolio and showed Anemone the paintings she had already finished: the gay-colored thistle-finch and the blue titmouse, the kingfisher with plumage glittering like gems, the somber blackbird, the oriole and the green woodpecker.

"The trouble is," Aunt Gundula said, "the males are so conceited they want to be painted only in their wedding suits. Goodness, the trouble I have persuading them to sit for me in their ordinary everyday feathers."

As she talked Aunt Gundula went on with her painting. "This is going to be the busiest time of year for me," she said. "And not only on account of the Easter eggs. The birds of passage will be back before long. The starlings and blackbirds are here already, and I can hardly wait for all the others. But I worry for them, Anemone, worry terribly. There have never been so many birds of prey around as this winter. They've even been bold enough to attack the hens and pigeons—why, the cathedral pigeon flock is only half its usual size. The poor darlings keep fluttering in at my window half dead with terror. Even my bees are uneasy. All nature seems to be in an uproar, just like the world of human beings."

"Yet it used to be so peaceful here in Vogelsang," Anemone said thoughtfully. "And now even I can't get along with Papa."

"You're right, it never used to be like this. Everything has been turned topsy-turvy in our good old town lately. Think of our poor friends, the Trippstrills and Winkel-risses—without anything to live on and hardly enough to eat, and who knows what is going to happen when they are brought to trial. They're accused of stealing the stone maiden. According to the mayor, they've gone and sold it to some museum in one of the neighboring towns. Have you ever heard the like—accusing honest people of a crime without the slightest shred of evidence. It's a frightful injustice!"

"Tyranny," Anemone said, "just like Papa."

"Well, maybe the mayor wanted to get rid of your two uncles so that he can give their jobs to his own friends. They were always a thorn in his side because they kept voting against him in the Town Council. They had to—what honorable man could look on and not protest when more and more of the people's old rights were being taken away. Even the songbirds who have always been our dear guests are caught in nets for roasting! Who ever heard of controls on beekeepers, chicken raisers and pigeon fanciers in a free city! The way the mayor has worked it, half of all their produce has to be turned in so that this fat glutton and his councilors can stuff themselves on eggs and honey. But things can't go on this way. If the men of Vogelsang are willing to swallow all this, his honor the mayor will learn what the womenfolk can do!"

"Absolutely!" Anemone cried enthusiastically. "We'll have a revolution so that Uncle Trippstrill and Winkelriss and Eusebius get their jobs back and the poor birds won't be trapped in nets any more. And so that there'll be enough eggs for Easter, because we need an awful lot, don't we? We've just had the French Revolution in school. I can look it up in my history book and see how they did it."

"French Revolution?" Gundula said. "Well, as a matter of fact—I'm not so keen on revolutions. I'd rather see it done without violence and bloodshed."

During this conversation it had been growing pitch-dark outside. Black clouds marched across the sky, and the delicate silver crescent of a moon showed through their chinks only now and then. There was dense silence in Cathedral Square below them. There were no more voices or hammer blows. One window after the other glowed with light in the houses across the square, and suddenly Anemone exclaimed: "Look, Aunt Gundula, Uncle Eusebius has just turned on his lamp."

"Oh, him!" Gundula said. "He thinks his one lamp can light up the whole square—that Mister Smart Aleck and round-the-world traveler. Knows all there is to know, of course, and tries to tell experienced people all kinds of nonsense about our native birds."

"Why are you mad at poor Uncle Eusebius, Aunt Gundula?" Anemone exclaimed. "And he's having such a hard time now that the mayor has fired him!"

"His life could be a lot better if he wanted it to. Does he have to be such an awful womanhating old bachelor going around with unironed shirts and half the buttons off his coat? But it's none of my affair!" And whisk! She drew the curtains so close that not the tiniest ray of light from Eusebius's lamp could find its way into the room.

"But I am very fond of him," Anemone said firmly. She had her likes and dislikes, and she clung to her opinions in spite of what others might say.

"Is that so?" Gundula said with her nose in the air. "Now suppose you take yourself off to bed, Miss Florus. Little girls have a way of getting pert when their elders let them stay up too late."

Whereupon she opened the door to the adjoining room which Anemone had never yet seen because she had only come on daytime visits.

There stood a huge bed with pillows piled high, and enclosed with billowing hangings which Aunt Gundula had covered with needlework. These curtains were more beautiful than the loveliest picture book. All along the lower hem there were fish, shellfish, and all kinds of strange-looking deep-sea creatures swimming about among gardens of coral and green seaweed. The mid-section was devoted to the solid world of stones and the lively world of plants and animals. Here gems flashed sparkling colors, flowers of every description budded and blossomed, animals of many kinds leaped or crouched, while above their heads flew glinting birds, butterflies and beetles. Way up at the top was the sun, flanked by planets and the signs of the zodiac. It was all so enter-taining that Anemone completely forgot how tired she was. But the strangest part of it all was that high up, at the very mid-point of the canopy, was perched Gundula's beehive, humming incessantly on a deep note.

"The humming puts you to sleep faster than anything," Gundula said. "And now let's find you a nightgown."

From one of her fat-bellied chests of drawers she took a nightgown just about twice as wide and long as Anemone, who slipped into it, giggling delightedly, while Gundula donned its exact mate. Then she helped the child climb up into the high bed. "All aboard!" she cried. "The Dream Ship is sailing in a minute." She clapped her hands, whereupon the bird and the animals left the studio and came to the bedroom. Lora flew up to the curtain pole, gave one more strident cry: "Come in unless you're a man!", tucked her head under her bright wing and composed her feathers. Minette strolled in slowly, hon-oring her guest Winnie by permitting her to enter first. Snow White, the mouse, followed them, and the three curled up cozily beside one another in a basket lined with pink silk. The bees which had been lingering on the crocuses came zooming into the room and popped inside the hive. The low humming struck a deeper and deeper note.

Aunt Gundula clambered up into the Dream Ship beside Anemone. "Tomorrow we'll paint Easter eggs," she said. "Now close your eyes and go to sleep and not another word out of you." Then she spread an array of writing materials out on the blanket and began writing, with pen flying.

"Why do you write in bed?" Anemone could not help asking.

"Good night!" Aunt Gundula said emphatically. "No more chatter if you please. Hm. Why do I write in bed? That's the best place to concentrate. The bees are humming above us, the pigeons are cooing in the gable and the pen runs along by itself. But now go to sleep."

"Good night, Aunt Gundula," Anemone said. She would have liked to ask half a dozen more questions. She was quite certain she would not be able to fall asleep because she felt so awfully bad about her papa's being so unfair to her.

The bees hummed. The pigeons cooed. The big pillows were like white sails smelling of sea and summer and sunlight. And now the cathedral clock began to ring the hour, and all the other clocks in the many towers of the town answered it. When the ringing stopped, only the soft scratching of pen over paper could be heard. Gently the Dream Ship sailed over the roofs, and in spite of feeling bad Anemone was already fast asleep.

Perdu

WE HAVE TO make some money," Anemone confided to Winnie next morning as she worked over the dog's silken pelt with comb and brush. "Aunt Gundula is pretty poor. Today I'll help paint Easter eggs and tomorrow we'll sell them in the marketplace. We have to be careful not to let old Schlummermutz catch us, because then he'll ask us where the eggs came from and all the nice farm women will be in a pretty pickle."

Winnie thought she had had enough of combing and brushing. She shook her head so hard that her beautifully groomed beard became tousled and had to be combed over again. "You see!" Anemone said sternly. Then she sat down to breakfast with Aunt Gundula, while Winnie, Minette and Snow White lapped fresh milk and zwieback.

A feeble streak of March sunlight splashed across the white tablecloth, but otherwise it looked pretty raw and wintry outside, which made the room feel all the more cozy. Fragrant steam rose from the flowered coffee pot; crisp hard rolls and crescents and soft brown biscuits were heaped up in a bowl. The baker's boy had brought these at daybreak. He whistled downstairs every morning, at which Gundula would lower her basket on a long cord and pull it up again laden with hot rolls, the morning newspaper and a bottle of milk. She was already deep in the newspaper, hidden completely behind it, so that Anemone could only guess her presence from the sounds of amazement, amusement or annoyance that came from behind the rustling pages. Above the window a tiny shutter had been opened, and through this a titmouse or a finch came flying in every so often to pick up a few crumbs from the table. Pigeons came too for the corn which Aunt Gundula kept in a bowl beside her coffee cup. Anemone was delighted with these trusting visitors, who settled on Gundula's shoulders and sat twittering for a while. As they twittered Gundula would occasionally nod or shake her head or frown.

Suddenly her face emerged from behind the newspaper and she pointed her forefinger at a certain spot on the page. "Here is something for us, Anemone," she said, and Anemone read the following notice:

LOST!

Mr. Benjamin Florus reports the disappearance yesterday evening, from his home, of his daughter Anemone and her dog Winnie. Kidnapping is feared. But possibly the child ran away and is hiding. The Town Constabulary Force requests any information that may lead to her recovery. A large reward is offered to anyone who can supply information and/or produce the missing child or dog. The girl is eleven years old, has a long, very thick pigtail and a pug nose. Last seen, she was wearing a blue coat and red cap. The dog is gray and extremely snappy. Caution! It will not permit its mistress to be touched.

Anemone sat thunderstruck. Then she murmured in an injured voice: "There, you can see Papa doesn't love me any more. Otherwise how could he put that about a pug nose in the newspaper. And calling Winnie snappy in public."

"Now, Anemone, don't be silly! That's just the kind of notice Ilsebill would make up. Probably your father was so upset about your disappearance that she decided to put an ad in the newspaper."

"You won't turn us in, will you?" Anemone asked, giving her aunt a pleading look. "It wouldn't be any use, because I just won't go home."

"Stubborn, aren't we!" Aunt Gundula said. "But don't worry, I'm not going to turn you in because I'd rather have you where I can keep an eye on you than think of you running around Heaven knows where and getting into mischief. If I only knew what to do with you. You won't like being cooped up in here for very long. . . ."

"Of course not," Anemone said. "I want to go out and sell Easter eggs."

"Sell Easter eggs, do you? How do you think that is going to work out? Schlummermutz would take you by the collar and drag you right back to Ilsebill. And what about Winnie? She can't go walking on roofs like Minette, and she would be spotted in a minute because she's the only Kerry in town."

"I'd like to see anybody try to catch her or grab hold

of me!" Anemone said fiercely. "Winnie would leap at their throats."

"Then first thing you know she would be shot. Our Chief Constable and his henchmen don't take any nonsense from a little dog. But we'll give them a run for their money. Come here, my lamb."

With one quick movement Aunt Gundula picked up a pair of shears—and snicksnack! Off came Anemone's pigtail. Anemone gasped. Her pigtail! The finest and thickest in school. But Aunt Gundula did not seem to care. "We'll just turn you into a boy," she said placidly. "Sexton's Emil is just about your size. Sexton's wife will lend me one of Emil's suits, and she won't let out a peep because I know where she hides the house key so that her husband can't go out to The Merry Finch evenings. Since he broke a leg on the cathedral steps coming home tipsy last year, she tries to keep him home. It's awfully convenient knowing someone's secret, when you want to trust her with one of your own."

Gundula went out. Her slippers could be heard clacking down the stairs and then slapping up again. When she came back, she found Anemone standing at the mirror looking at her close-cropped hair and trying to push the tip of her nose down with her finger.

"Here," Aunt Gundula said. "A pair of pants, a sweater and a warm jacket for going out. Hurry up, change your clothes; you can't do anything about that nose anyway. My elbow is twitching again; somebody's coming to call."

Anemone frowned at her aunt because of the remark about her nose. But she loved dressing up. All the boy's clothes fitted her to a T. "Fine," she said. "Now people can't tell me girls can't do this and girls mustn't do that. But what are we going to do with Winnie?"

Aunt Gundula put her finger to her nose and pondered.

"That's not so easy, not so easy," she murmured. But then she had an idea. She reached for her paint-box on the table by the window, selected the biggest brush, squeezed some paint on the palette and then clasped Winnie between her knees. Luckily the dog had been trimmed just a few days ago so that her pelt was like tight plush. On the gray background Aunt Gundula painted brown and black spots, tastefully distributed. She clipped off the fluffy socks on Winnie's legs with as little ceremony as she had cut off Anemone's braid. Winnie was disconcerted, but, since Anemone winked at her reassuringly, she was gentle and put up with it all. Before long she looked more like a piebald baby calf than a Kerry. Now Aunt Gundula picked up the shears to snip off her betraying beard, that mark of noble race. But Anemone cried out in horror and reached for the scissors so suddenly that her fingers were almost cut.

"Well, all right," Aunt Gundula said. "But if we don't clip it, we have to color it." She went into the kitchen, returned with a bowl of frosting to cover the sugar eggs, and with no more ado stuck Winnie's nose into it. "I'll have to make some more for the Easter eggs," she said.

The idea was wonderful; Winnie was utterly changed. But the effect didn't last long. Rolling her eyes with delight, the dog promptly licked off all the delicious icing. Anemone had to explain to her that from now on her beard would be colored before they left the house, and that she must not lick it off until they returned from their walk.

Minette-the-Cat and Snow White came closer to stare at the new Winnie. With head askew Lora peered down from her pole and seemed highly pleased. Then everybody went into the kitchen to prepare the eggs for painting.

On the table there were several dozen fresh hen's eggs, a basket of duck eggs and even a few large goose and turkey eggs. "Our dear mayor would have fits if he ever saw this," Aunt Gundula said smugly. She rolled up her sleeves. First the eggs had to be boiled and then dipped in soft pastel tints. Some Aunt Gundula left white; it depended on what background she needed for the decorations she was planning. Then some rich dough had to be mixed for pastry eggs.

Almonds were shelled and ground up for marzipan. The clever animals and the bird were allowed to help in this. Snow White delicately gnawed open the hazelnuts which were to be used for garnishing. She took each nut in her pink paws, gnawed through it rapidly with her sharp rodent's teeth, and let both halves of shell fall to either side of her. Then Minette reached out with her paw and swept the shells into the garbage can. Lora cracked the hard almonds with her strong beak. As a reward, both she and Snow White were entitled to eat every thirteenth nut. Anemone scalded the almonds and slipped off their brown skins, while Aunt Gundula worked the crushed nuts and pounded them into a wonderful marzipan paste in a glass bowl.

"How lucky that Lora has such a strong beak and Snow White such sharp teeth," Anemone said. "It saves us so much work."

"There are other advantages to that," Aunt Gundula said. "Constable Schlummermutz poked his nose in here a few days ago and wanted to inspect my hencoop. Lora, who can't stand men anyhow, swooped onto his shoulder and pecked at his cap. Meanwhile Snow White gnawed a hole in his boot and Minette humped up her back and stood at the door to the roof garden, where I keep my hens, spitting like a dragon. He mumbled something about a mistake and cleared right out. 'Humph, what a way to treat a municipal official,' I heard him grumbling all the way down the stairs. That's the last anybody came here inspecting my hens."

They heard footsteps on the stairs. "Your elbow!" Anemone said. "Here are your visitors already."

"That'll be Aunt Lena and Aunt Tina who come every year to help me paint the Easter eggs. Your mama used to come too."

"Come in unless you're a man!" Lora screeched, fluttering her wings. The bell in the vestibule tinkled. Anemone ran to open the door, and in came Lena Trippstrill and Tina Winkelriss, both somewhat out of breath from all the stairs. They weren't quite as slim as they used to be ten years ago when they had first started coming to Gundula's attic studio to help paint Easter eggs.

"Good morning," Aunt Tina said. "I hope you can use our help again, Gundula dear."

"I've been expecting you," Aunt Gundula said. "Everything is all set in the kitchen—we can start right away. I would be ashamed ever to show my face in town again if the children of Vogelsang were to get no eggs this Easter."

"Why, where did this lad come from?" Aunt Lena asked, raising her lorgnette to her eyes. "Have you engaged a baker's boy to help you with your errands?"

"Something of the sort," Aunt Gundula said, winking at Anemone. "He's going to sell my eggs in the market. His name is Perdu, by the way."

"Perdu," Aunt Lena said. "What an odd name."

"If I remember my French that means *lost*," Aunt Tina said.

"Yes," Aunt Gundula nodded. "He's half an orphan. So be nice to him."

The two aunts felt very sorry for the poor orphan child, and each of them fished in her purse for a tenpenny piece, so that the boy would be able to get himself a little treat when he went out to sell his eggs. A few pennies was all they themselves had in their purses because their husbands had been out of work for so long.

Then the three women went into the kitchen and Anemone, or rather Perdu, picked up a basket all neatly packed with eggs in soft moss, and went down to the market square, accompanied by Winnie.

"Be careful!" her aunts called after her. "And if anybody asks where you got the eggs..."

"Don't worry," Anemone waved back. "Nobody will ask me."

Among the booths in the big square there was already a great throng of children and grownups. That was good; one more boy would not be noticed. Wares were being cried; the succulent smoke from roasting pork sausages rose up toward the dove-gray spring sky. On the steps of the cathedral the flower-women sat among their baskets of narcissi, pussy willows, yellow primroses and blue grape-hyacinths. There were so many booths you didn't know where to turn first. Vogelsang's Easter market was famous all over the country. This year there was even a circus. A curious crowd was milling around in front of it, for a jolly clown was standing at the entrance to the tent, describing in the funniest way all the splendors inside. Not far away a marionette theater had been set up, and another crowd was gathered there because nothing of the kind had ever been seen in Vogelsang before. A beautifully painted sign announced in gigantic letters:

"Come in and see the true-to-life Comedy of Princess Lu Wi Seh, her three chamberlains and the dreadful Monster Wu, a story of the Land of the Chinese of more than one thousand years ago!"

Perdu sighed deeply. It *was* painful trying to decide whether to spend his twenty pennies on the circus or the marionette show. But first the eggs had to be disposed of. That went a good deal faster than he had expected, for as soon as he whispered to someone that he had some genuine Gundula Immofila eggs, the sale was made— after a cautious look around to make sure there was no constable nearby. Not that selling Easter eggs was exactly forbidden, but there might be trouble. After half a year of tyranny from the Town Hall, people were getting timid and fearful—which was something new for the merry, easy-going folk of Vogelsang.

As soon as the eggs were sold, Perdu was back at the space between the circus tent and the marionette theater, looking with longing eyes from one to the other. As he stood there undecidedly, someone behind him plucked his sleeve and said, "Hey, you, want to make some money?"

"Sure!" Perdu answered. The crowd was so thick here he could not manage to turn around at once.

"Listen," the voice went on. "I'm looking for a girl with a pug nose and an ugly gray mutt. Come and help me find her. I've got half a dozen fellows already. We'll have a lot of fun, and I'll pay everybody a mark each besides. How's about it?"

At this Perdu managed to whirl around sharply, and found himself facing the speaker. Sure enough it was Erwin, Ilsebill's darling Erwin, wearing his slyest, scampiest grin. Slap! and his cheek was stinging from a blow that had plenty of zip behind it because it was making up for all the slaps he should have received for a long time. For a moment the little pest's mouth flew open with surprise. "I'll help you find pugnosed girls and ugly mutts!" Perdu said bitterly. Erwin's own hand started to fly forward to return the blow when Winnie joined the fray. Her teeth took a good grip on his fat leg. Screaming, he ran off, hunting among the booths for his mama.

"I hope you didn't bite him very hard," Anemone said to her dog. "Well, what's done is done, and he certainly got what he deserves."

She turned her thoughts back to the circus. The fine horses were a terrible temptation. Besides, the colorful signs promised an elephant and a trained pig that was a real wonder. There were acrobats and clowns, and there was Blue Boy the Clever Dog who could read and count, and on the poster he looked very much like a Kerry. On the other hand the marionette theater seemed like a lot of fun too. A real Chinese princess and a monster were certainly worth looking at. Where to go, that was the question.

Suddenly Perdu felt his sleeve plucked again. His arm started to swing back, but just to be on the safe side he turned his head first and discovered that it was the clown.

"Peeps," the clown said, bowing.

"What peeps?" Perdu asked in astonishment.

"My name if you please, young gentleman. Peeps of Pampini's circus. Come here." He beckoned conspiratorily and drew Perdu to a corner of the circus tent, out of the crowd. "You have a remarkable animal with you. A dog, I should guess, though not of any breed I've ever seen. Would you mind my asking . . ."

"She's a Mongolerian Turkestan," Perdu informed him.

The clown seemed deeply impressed. "A Mong— Mongolerian Turkestan! Well, what do you know? Rare, very rare I imagine. I wonder if she is as smart as she looks? Can she jump, play dead and balance a piece of sugar on her nose until you tell her to eat it?"

"Nothing to it. She can do lots more than that."

"Not really! Then you must help us out of a fix, my

dear young gentleman. Our pig Rosalie cannot appear. She has become a mother, eight days before schedule. We were not expecting the blessed event until after Easter. It knocks a terrible hole in our program. Rosalie was our star number. We're ruined unless we can find a substitute.

"But my dog isn't a pig!" Perdu protested, offended.

"Far be it from me to imply anything of the sort," Peeps reassured him. "I am lost in admiration of your extraordinarily animal. And therefore I beg you, I implore you ... We will pay whatever you ask."

Pay? That was just what Perdu needed. He looked questioningly at Winnie, and she wagged her tail in agreement. "You must understand," Perdu said, "that you are speaking of Lady Pooh of Carlingford Lough, daughter of the farfamed Skilligaly who wore the Great Star of the Crystal Palace on his collar. No one has ever dared to suggest to her that she perform in a circus. I don't know but what her aristocratic family might object." Anemone loved to use words and phrases from the many books she had read.

"Of course," Peeps said, "I can well understand that, my young friend. But who can afford to consider family prejudices of that sort nowadays. I would never have presumed to make any such proposal if I were not driven to it by our present predicament. Please come with me and talk to Director Pampini. You will find him a very kind man and a true animal lover. We ought to have a short rehearsal right away, since the performance starts in half an hour. If the rehearsal is satisfactory we will pay you a whole taler, and of course rations for Lady Pooh, and for you free admission to the circus as often as you like."

Perdu was feeling almost dizzy by now. It was all too wonderful to grasp at once. "A taler ... You mean a taler *every* day?" he asked uncertainly.

"I mean a taler every *show,* and we have two shows a day."

Perdu was dumbstruck; this was too much for words. He would be able to go to the circus as often as he liked, and not only go in free, but receive pay besides.

They found the director in his office, his hair tousled, despair written all over his face. "Eleven sucklings!" he moaned. "I always thought Rosalie was a good trouper and then she does this to me. Eleven piglets in the straw beside her, and now she has to feed her babies and can't appear. Couldn't she wait until after Easter? The public is crazy about her. Oh, I'm a ruined man."

"By no means, sir," the clown spoke up cheerfully. "I've saved the day, boss. Here you see Lady Pooh of I-don't-know-where, a genuine Turkestanian Mongerel. Very rare and awfully smart, I am told."

"A Turkestanian what?" Mr. Pampini asked. "This isn't the time for silly jokes, Peeps!"

"A Monglerian Turkestan," Perdu corrected, with modest pride. "Straight from England."

And Winnie with her painted spots came forward and stood in front of the troubled gentleman. She certainly was a sight to mend the broken heart of a circus director. Had anyone ever seen a dog like this before? The coat of black and chocolate-brown spots against the silvery gray background was very distinguished-looking. But the beard was simply magnificent. Snowy and glittering as though made of needle-sharp icicles, it stood out around the charming shiny black nose and dark cherry eyes that glowed slyly as if to say, "Don't worry, we'll take care of things."

Perdu heard the director give an enormous sigh of relief. "Rehearse!" he said excitedly. "Hurry up, let's have a rehearsal, Peeps. Not Rosalie's program, of course. But what will it be? Let's try the dog with Bijou. Pronto!"

They rushed back of the tent where the circus wagons were arranged in a large square. A chestnut pony wearing a white leather saddle was led out, and the director called upon Winnie to ride the horse.

Winnie looked at Anemone. Anemone nodded encouragingly to Winnie. Then, with one bold leap, the dog jumped up into the saddle. She would just as unhesitatingly have jumped in front of a locomotive if her mistress had asked her to. A light slap on the crupper and the pony began tearing around the ring. Winnie looked a little worried at first, but luckily the saddle was arranged so that she could hold onto it, and after a few times around she began enjoying the ride. Whoosh! the pony took a hurdle. Winnie managed to hang on. Then Bijou rose up on her hind legs and pranced around a bit. This time Winnie was hard put to it not to slide off. But from moment to moment she became surer of herself. At the end she was barking merrily each time the pony took one of its gay leaps.

"Bravo!" the director cried out, blowing a kiss at Winnie. "Magnifico! A born equestrian artist. Can she retrieve too? Will she be afraid to jump through a burning hoop?"

"She's never been afraid of anything," Perdu said. "Not even of darning needles. And she does everything I tell her to."

The band was already striking up its gay march and people began pouring into the circus tent. Perdu stroked Winnie once more and implored her to do her best. But there was nothing to worry about. Winnie already seemed to be on the best of terms with the pony, and she behaved as if she were altogether in her element. Bijou shook her silken mane, tossed the ostrich plumes ornamenting her head and made the silver bells on her saddle girth ring merrily as she whirled once more around herself and then flew off in time to the music, her dashing rider firmly in the saddle.

"And you, my esteemed young man, come along to my box," the director said, giving Perdu's hand a long, grateful shake. "Please sit right up front at the railing so that Lady Pooh can see you and won't get stage fright."

And so instead of sitting in a twenty-penny seat in the last row, Perdu sat at the very front in the director's box, and when he saw Winnie galloping by he raised his hand to show her that he was there.

"Can I do you a favor?" Mr. Pampini whispered in Perdu's ear. "Ask for anything you want."

"I'd love to have a ride on the elephant," Perdu said, and he pinched his arm to make sure he was not dreaming.

Troubles, Troubles,
Troubles!

GUNDULA, LENA AND Tina were so hard at work in the
little kitchen that their brows were beaded with perspiration. The shelves were already covered with row upon
row of eggs; eggs of pastry and marzipan, snow-white
sugar eggs and hard-boiled hen, goose and turkey eggs.
Each of the women had taken over some of the work.
Lena had shaped the marzipan eggs and popped the pastry
eggs into the oven. Tina was busy stirring up sugar icing
and chocolate frosting.

But now came the nicest part of the job. Gundula
started decorating her eggs. First she used the pastry-tubes
to spray fantastic curlicues on the smooth surfaces of the
marzipan and sugar eggs. Then she drew all kinds of
flowers and animals, lettered pretty proverbs and dabbed
in bright spots of color with her paintbrush. Next step
was to press almonds, raisins and hazelnuts into the soft
bodies of the eggs. The creations she turned out could

not be duplicated by the best confectioners in the town.
There were hen eggs painted with roses and forget-me-
not drops. On others curly-wooled Easter lambs were playing
among buttercups in green meadows, or a trio of bright
birds were perching upon a flowering branch with tiny
bees hovering among the blossoms. Or baby rabbits were
hopping about in the grass and fluffy yellow chicks slipping under the wings of the mother hen.

There were also eggs on which only a single bird was
painted. There were the eggs Gundula Immofila really
owed her fame to, for the birds were painted so artistically
that people never tired of looking at them. Very few
children could ever make up their minds to eat one of
these precious creations. In most of the parlors of
Vogelsang you would find one or more of Gundula's eggs
in the place of honor inside the china closet—right beside
the withered wreath Mama had worn to her wedding, or
the flower-picture made out of Aunt Elfriede's hair, or
the ash-tray showing Mount Vesuvius that Uncle Albert
had brought back from his famous trip to Naples.

Every year the whole town tried to guess what motif
Gundula would paint on her eggs. And all the children
were set on having report cards for Easter, so that they
would be given one or two of Gundula's wonderful eggs.

When all but one of the eggs were beautifully painted
and lined up on the shelves, Gundula took the last one—
a very large and smooth goose egg. She looked mourn-
fully at it for a moment and began mixing her colors
afresh. Her two friends threw one another knowing
glances; from years of experience they knew that this
one would be Gundula's masterpiece, and that there was
something very special about it. Pushing aside the bowls
of icing, the baking tins and rolling pins, they looked on

respectfully as Gundula set about her work with brush and paints. As she went on her expression grew more and more pathetic.

At last the picture was finished, and it was truly something to behold. Under a flowering linden tree stood a girl in a pink dress and a young man in a chocolate-colored suit, holding hands. All around them the landscape was bursting into blossom, and in the branches of the tree perched twittering birds. Below the picture, painted in graceful, fancy letters, was the word: UNFORGOTTEN!

During their work the three women had not uttered a single sound. But after Gundula had washed her brushes, Lena asked timidly: "What do you do every year with this last one—your most beautiful egg?"

"What an indiscreet question!" Tina said, darting a look at Lena to silence her.

"I don't mind your asking," Gundula said. "You don't think I would waste it on that monster, do you? No, sir! Every year on Easter morning I break it. I love to see the shell go splintering to bits. And then..."

"Then?" her two friends asked in suspense.

"Why, then I eat it, every last morsel of it, just like any ordinary egg."

Then Gundula took Lena and Tina into the studio where the coffee table was already set with her finest Meissner cups. Their work was done for today and now they had a chance to chat about this and that.

"Men!" Tina Winkelriss sighed after she had finished her second cup of coffee. "They *are* a cross. Day and night we wear ourselves out slaving for them, and what do we get for it? Rank ingratitude!"

"You too?" Lena also gave a downcast sigh.

Tina nodded. "No need to keep it from you two, my

dearest friends. I'm terribly worried about Agamemnon."

"Rafael, too, is so changed lately," Lena confessed. In her velvety brown eyes, which were usually so gentle and affectionate, there was a spark of righteous anger. "He has *secrets*. And if there's anything I can't stand it's secrets."

"So has Agamemnon." Tina declared. "My dears, you can't imagine all the trouble I've been having with him. Ever since the disappearance of that stone statue and the mayor's firing him there hasn't been a moment's peace or pleasantness in our home. And wouldn't you think husband and wife should stick closer together than ever in hard times. If only he'd listened to my advice we would have been spared all of this. As soon as I heard about it I told him: 'Keep your hands off those statues, Agi. Who cares if they look their age? I'm not getting any younger myself, and nobody's offered to restore me.' It's just one of the new mayor's crazy ideas, I told him. But no, he wouldn't listen to me. Those maidens had to come down out of their niches, no matter what. Deposited them in the vestry, they did, and that's where the men were all day long, for weeks on end, watching the workmen who went over the statues with all kinds of fancy tools. Agamemnon kept raving about how fine the statues were now, and after all we owed something to a famous old cathedral like ours, he said, and not a town far and wide had such beautifully restored works of art, and it would bring the tourists in and so on and so on. And what does it all come down to but one of the statues missing and a waterspout too, wouldn't you know it?" Tina concluded, somewhat breathless after her long speech.

Gradually the whole sad story came to light. Lena and Tina talked in turn while Gundula listened attentively, only now and then tossing in some remark such as: "Of course, that was bound to happen," or: "I would have expected that!" Or else she would only shake her head, look up at the ceiling and go: "Tsk, tsk!"

Every since the disappearance of the stone maiden, the two husbands had been different men. At first they seemed to be giving themselves up to the bleakest despair over the loss of their positions and, worse still, of their good names. Rafael Trippstrill, a quiet person by nature, sank into gloomy brooding and lost weight steadily. Agamemnon Winkelriss, who had quite a different temperament, had turned crotchety and was full of prophecies of doom. One misfortune would follow another, he assured his alarmed wife. Life was always like that. They were already poor and without income. So far, so bad. But wait until they were brought to trial—they might as well give up hope. Everybody knew that the mayor had it in for them for opposing him in the town council. Now they would be accused not only of embezzling town property, but of high treason also. Poor Tina began dreaming nights of the rack and gallows. And more than once Agamemnon woke her up to say that he wanted to make his will right away, because he felt certain he would be condemned to death.

"But the two of them are innocent," Gundula interjected. "Nobody believes for a minute that they had anything to do with the stone maiden's disappearance."

"So I've told Rafael a hundred times," Lena declared. "But he tells me that's all very well, but how are they going to *prove* their innocence."

So it had gone for quite a while, and the worried, patient wives had done their best from morning to night to cheer up their husbands. But then, four or five weeks ago, something had come over the men. At first their wives were pleased to see them no longer sitting around the house all day, lost in sad thoughts. For they did seem to be doing something at last. There was a great deal of going to and fro between the Trippstrill and the Winkelriss houses, and Eusebius, too, was drawn into the conferences on how to find the missing maiden. Not that it seemed likely he would come up with any sensible ideas. In fact, with his fondness for mischief and practical jokes he might very well get all of them into a worse mess than ever. But he, too, was almost as badly off as the other two families. He could no longer pay the cleaning woman who ordinarily came in once a week to take care of dust and spiderwebs in his apartment.

At any rate, the three men had been putting their heads together, but so far nothing much seemed to have come of their conferences. But strangely enough, they began again to look quite chipper and satisfied with themselves. This past week, in fact, they had been actually gay, although there was no apparent reason for their high spirits. They had taken to staying out all night without giving their wives the slightest hint as to what they were about. When questioned they made vague and unbelievable excuses, said their wives ought to trust them and everything would turn out all right; they had their reasons for keeping their plans to themselves for the present.

Whatever these plans were, the niche on the west wing of the cathedral was still empty. Easter was coming closer and closer, and with it the day they were due to be brought to trial.

"I just won't stand for it any longer," Tina said. "I've had enough. I'm willing to stick by him through hard times, but I can't bear all these secrets. Stubbornness, I call it, hidebound stubbornness. If you don't mind, Gundula dear, I'd like to stay here." From her bag she took a toothbrush and nightcap and laid them on the table. Lena silently followed her example.

Gundula pressed their hands and said, "My dear, you are welcome to stay with me as long as you like. There's room enough in my Dream Ship. But it saddens me to think that even your peaceful homes are affected by the bad temper and ill will that seem to be all over our town nowadays. It's as though people were under an evil spell. Old friendships are going to pot, children running away from home and wives breaking up with their husbands. You know even I have quarreled with my old friends in the Bird Club. All Eusebius's fault, if you know what I mean. In January I lectured on the horned owls, screech owls, hoot owls and crows that have been swarming in this part of the country lately and doing so much damage to our useful songbirds and our pigeons and hens. I said that there was something altogether uncanny about it and that the frightful screech which comes from the cathedral towers night after night cannot possibly be the voice of an ordinary owl. Then Eusebius got up and with that superior smile of his said that it was too bad the esteemed lecturer should make statements she could not possibly prove, and after all a club of bird lovers and students of nature had to stick to the firm ground of science. *Even* here in Vogelsang, he went on, sneeringly. But of course, he said, you couldn't expect logical thinking from a woman, talented in other ways though she might be."

"Logical thinking!" Tina said with great indignation. "Did you ever hear anything so silly. That's just what you can expect when a man goes gadding about the world for three years and loses all feeling for his home town."

"I feel almost sorry for him," said Lena, who had a quieter and gentler nature than Tina's. "However, he should know this isn't the first time a ghostly owl's screech has been heard from the cathedral towers every night. What about the time the poisonous henbane turned all of Vogelsang upside down?"

"Henbane?" her friends asked in amazement. "What are you talking about?"

Lena hesitated for a moment. Then she began: "You know that I haven't spent all my life knitting socks and standing over a hot stove. Incidentally, many years ago, I wrote my doctoral thesis on the statues in the west wing of the cathedral. So I know those stone maidens better than anyone else in this town, including Trippstrill with all his learning. That was why I told him to look out when the whole business started, just as you warned Agememnon, Tina. Only *I* knew exactly what there was to look out for. Take care, Rafael, I told him again and again, or they'll play a trick on you. They have their ways, especially the one that stands under the waterspout. You see, in doing my thesis I had to read the old chronicles that no one bothers with nowadays. And one of the chronicles tells the story of how this same foolish virgin disappeared, three hundred years ago when our town was governed by a robber knight who was called the Wicked Owl, one of the darkest tyrants of history."

"Not really!" Tina gasped, but Gundula just nodded her head and, oddly enough, looked rather pleased.

"Take my word for it," Tina continued. "And what should I find carved upon her pedestal but a picture of a little plant. The carving is very tiny and worn away by the rain of centuries. But worn as it is, there's no doubt that the plant is henbane, or witches' weed. I pointed all this out to Rafael, but do you think it made any impression on him? Not even when the trouble did start, just as I predicted, did he admit that I knew better."

"Who would expect a man ever to realize he was wrong and say so?" Gundula said. "Look at how Eusebius has behaved. Ten years ago he came here every evening for a whole winter, enjoyed the hospitality of my warm room, devoured mountains of gingerbread and drank gallons of mulled punch while we worked together on the big bird book. We were one heart and one soul, and we agreed on all the problems of bird lore, too. Our names were to appear jointly on the title page of our book, *The Birds of Vogelsang,* and it never occurred to me to doubt that we two would be united for the rest of our lives in all other respects. But when spring came Eusebius packed his knapsack, said so-long, and off he went on this silly trip around the world. For three years he stayed away. At the beginning he sent a good many picture postcards with some of his funny verses on them. They are all in that drawer there, but I haven't looked at them for years. Then the cards stopped coming, and one fine day he turned up again as if he'd just been over the hills to the next village, and was flabbergasted when I didn't throw my arms around his neck. But I told him right out what I thought of him, and since then we've kept out of each other's way. The only times we meet are at the Bird Club. And now I can tell you I intend to stay away from there, too, after what I had to put up with from him. I don't care a pin for him and the whole Bird Club any longer."

Lena and Tina nodded agreement. Of course Gundula was right—she couldn't go on taking that kind of insolence from a man who had been away from Vogelsang so long that he could hardly be considered a Vogelsanger any more. Queer and warped ideas, that's what came of traveling around. Why should anyone who was fortunate enough to live in Vogelsang want to go traveling?

"And consider our friend Benjamin Florus," Gundula went on. "There you have another fine example of how blind men are. His late wife was the finest woman in the world. And now he's taken this frightful person with her rascal of a son into his house and lets her wind him around her finger with dumplings and cream puffs and the way she blinks her eyes. I'll bet she'll end up as Mrs. Florus one of these days. She's driven all our poor deceased friend's animals out of the house, those she hasn't killed yet, that is. Not a bird will nest in the Florus gardens this year, not a bee will fertilize his flowers, and since yesterday even Anemone has left her father's house."

"You don't say!" the two women exclaimed with one voice.

"Didn't you read the notice in the newspaper?" Gundula asked, forgetting that as a thrift measure, the two had had their subscription to the newspaper stopped. "Here, look at this."

"My goodness!" Lena exclaimed. "Oh, the poor, sweet child. And that darling dog who used to be so devoted to Anemone's mother. Where do you think the two of them can be? Why, it would be just terrible if they were found and delivered into the hands of that wicked woman and her nasty boy again."

"If only they would come to you, Gundula," Tina said. "Here they would be safe and well taken care of."

"That's just what they have done—come to me," Gundula said. And then she told her friends all about the darning needle and the ear, and what had come of it.

When Anemone returned from the market, both aunts fell upon her and hugged and kissed her—a procedure that seemed entirely unnecessary to Anemone but which she put up with patiently enough. Winnie meanwhile licked the sugar off her bread, with help from Minette and Snow White. After Anemone had wriggled free from her aunts' embraces she took a taler from her pocket and laid it on the table. "This is what Winnie earned," she said, "and here's the money for the eggs, too." She dug into her jacket pocket and took out a handful of small coins. "Winnie is going to earn twice this every day from now on, only you have to let us leave again from eight to ten, because there are two performances every day, one at four and one at eight. Winnie's getting free food, too, pork chops, if you please, and I rode on an elephant. His name is Kim and he's the sweetest thing."

"Wait a minute!" her aunts cried—grownups are rather slow about taking in a lot of exciting adventures all at once. "Please go a little slower. Two talers a day is wonderful. With that and the egg money the four of us can get along very nicely. Because we are staying here, Anemone. For—hm—all sorts of reasons."

"Fine," Anemone said, not particularly impressed by this news. There was too much she had to tell about. "First we ran into Erwin. He talked pretty fresh so I couldn't help slapping him, and Winnie just nipped him a tiny bit. But he didn't recognize either of us, Aunt Gundula—you don't have to make such a face. Then the clown said to me, My dear young gentleman, he said, meaning me, come along and see our director. Rosalie has eleven babies and can't perform. And your dog is a very rare specimen, he said, her appearance alone will stir up the crowd, Just think the clown said young gentleman to me..."

"Wait a minute!" the three aunts exclaimed again. "What clown was this and who is Rosalie? Our heads are simply whirling."

"Why, the clown from Pampini's circus, of course. Who else? And Rosalie is the performing pig. I saw her piglets, they look like they were made of pink marzipan, they're beautiful. But they came eight days too soon. On account of the strain of traveling, Peeps says."

"Yes, yes, but what about Winnie? What has all this

to do with Winnie and the two talers?"

Anemone made an effort to tell her story all over again for the benefit of her aunts. "Winnie took Rosalie's place, don't you understand? She rode on the pony and the audience was just stunned. Later she jumped through three flaming hoops, without the pony, just like that; she thought nothing of it because I was in the director's box and winked at her. And while the other numbers were going on we practiced something in the horse tent—a big scene with Peeps. Winnie imitated a trained lion like she really was one. She rolled her eyes, struck out with her paws, gnashed her teeth and growled. The clown pretended like he was scared to death of the lion and stood there with his knees knocking together. But there was no help for it, he couldn't get out of fighting the lion and the lion sunk his teeth into one of the clown's wide trouser legs and dragged him all around the ring. And even though the clown kept going bang-bang something terrible with a gun, the lion beat him. And you should have seen the lion sitting proudly on the clown's body and the clown dead as a doornail. The people in the audience were rolling in the aisles, and the children went wild. They clapped and shouted and screamed: Again, do it again! And they threw candy and chocolate into the ring so it was dropping around Winnie like hail. But Winnie ate only a little of it; she left most of it for Rosalie, because she's just had babies, and for the artists' children, and I had a little too. The director was overwhelmed, absolutely. He kept kissing his fingers and crying: "Bene!" and "Molto bene" and some other words—I wish I could remember them. And afterwards he offered me a thousand talers for Winnie, but of course I laughed in his face."

After Anemone had finished her long story and Winnie

had been properly praised and petted by everybody, they sat down to supper. There were potato pancakes. When Anemone had finished her sixth, she began looking around the room and her eyes lit on the big egg on the chest of drawers.

"What a marvelous egg!" she exclaimed. "Whose is it?"

"My own," Aunt Gundula said. "Am I not allowed to paint an egg for myself?"

"Of course you are," Anemone answered. "Please excuse me from table before you're through. I must get a look at that egg." She went over to the chest and peered. "May I light the candles?" she asked over her shoulder.

"If you like," Aunt Gundula replied.

There was a silence for some seconds after the bright flames of the candles shot into the air. Then Anemone spoke again, this time almost whispering in admiration: "Ooooooh! Molto bene! Absolutely! The pink girl looks like you, Aunt Gundula, maybe a little younger. And the chocolate man—why, that's the spitting image of Uncle Eusebius." Anemone giggled. "Isn't that funny!"

"What strikes you as so funny?" Aunt Gundula said rather tartly. "I can pick my models wherever I please, can't I?"

Certainly she could. But why she suddenly turned so red was a mystery to Anemone. First she was mad at Uncle Eusebius on account of his going abroad, and then she painted his picture on the egg and blushed when you made an innocent remark about it. Queer!

By now it was a quarter to eight and time to report to the circus. "Come, Winnie," Anemone said. "You can't go to sleep yet. You're a working woman."

"Oh, dear, what a shame," soft-hearted Aunt Lena lamented. "To think the poor child has to go out in the dark of night to earn money for us."

"I love it," Anemone said, and she crammed the boy's cap on her head. "That egg is a honey, Aunt Gundula. Honestly!" And she was out of the door.

"Be careful on the stairs," Aunt Lena called after her. But Anemone never used the stairs. She always slid down the bannisters.

"And for Heaven's sake don't let anyone catch you," Aunt Gundula warned.

When Anemone and Winnie returned at five after ten—both of them good and tired by now—they found the three aunts still sitting at the table in the studio, deep in grave conversation.

"Be a good girl and take a look outside to make sure the hencoop is shut tight," Aunt Gundula requested her. "Take Minette along."

To get to the tiny roof garden where Gundula kept her hens you had to climb out the kitchen window. It was a lovely place. Later on, tulips and daffodils would be blooming in all the corners. Their first green tips were already thrusting out of the black soil. There were also several rose bushes and a young plum tree. Anemone found the hencoop securely shut, and she was about to clamber back through the window when Minette suddenly began to spit. She arched her back and stared up at the dark sky with luminous eyes. What was that, floating up above like a dense thundercloud? "Aunt Gundula!" Anemone called through the open window. "Look, Minette is spitting at a big cloud."

The three aunts rushed to the window and looked up at the sky. There was the cloud, hovering black and sinister over the town. But a closer look showed it to be a swarm of huge birds circling around the towers of the cathedral, from which came a ghostly, long-drawn-out owl's hooting.

"Those night birds again," Gundula said, shaking her head.

"It makes me think of the Wicked Owl you have been mentioning," Tina remarked.

"The Wicked Owl?" Anemone said with sparkling eyes. "Who is he?"

"Just an old tyrant," Gundula said, "who had Vogelsang under his thumb a few hundred years ago."

"Tell me a story about him," Anemone pleaded. "Oh, please, auntie, do."

But the aunts were not in a mood for telling stories. Silently and thoughtfully they undressed for the night. Lena and Tina were each given one of Gundula's ample nightgowns from the fat-bellied chest, and by and by they all boarded the Dream Ship. Anemone and Gundula lay with their heads at the head of the bed, and Lena and Tina with their heads at the foot. The Dream Ship was so wide and long that there was plenty of room for all.

"I still have to do some writing," Aunt Gundula said when they were all in bed. She lit a candle, reached for her pen and tablet, and started a new chapter. Anemone, whose curiosity was greater than her weariness, peered over at the paper and saw the heading:

"ON THE DANGER OF THE NOCTURNAL BIRDS AND THE FALLACIOUSNESS OF SO-CALLED LOGICAL THINKING

Hitherto we have managed very well in our good old town without logical thinking, and we will do best to leave it to towns like Nowhere and Somewhere."

Anemone read only this far when Aunt Gundula whispered to her: "Sleep, Miss Nosy. You've had a hard day."

"But a nice one," Anemone murmured. "And isn't Winnie the best and smartest dog in the world? Good night, Aunt Gundula. Good night, Winnie darling, my wonder dog. Tomorrow we'll go to the circus again."

Anemone's Dream

As EVERYONE KNOWS, there are people who can understand the language of plants and animals in their dreams. It is as if they return to a long-lost paradise where all creatures live side by side like brothers and all understand one another. There lions do not eat lambs, but feed on grass and fruit. Birds of prey do not pounce on smaller birds, scorpions and tarantulas do not sting, and even snakes have no poison fangs and do no one any harm.

Anemone was so tired after all the excitement of the day that she fell asleep at once. She thought she felt something tickling her ear and murmured sleepily, "Go back to your basket, Winnie. Why are you tickling me with your beard?"

"Because I have to speak with you," Winnie said very plainly.

All at once Anemone noticed that she was no longer lying in Aunt Gundula's huge bed. The Dream Ship had let her off somewhere. Oh, this was the garden of the old Florus house, and Anemone was standing in one of the beds of gay, sweet-scented spring flowers. Her father was going about the garden, picking off a withered leaf here, setting a shrub to rights there. At last he stopped in front of Anemone. "We must breed out that pugnose," he said. "Then she'll really be perfect." Anemone was about to answer, but it was no longer her father standing in front of her; it was naughty Erwin. He called something to Ilsebill who was leaning out of the topmost window of the house and shooing the pigeons who were perching on the ridge of the roof, as had been their hereditary right ever since the Floruses had lived here.

"Shall I pluck up the Anemone?" Erwin called to Ilsebill. And she nodded, laughing, and called out several times: "Pluck it out, Erwin, my pet. Pluck it out, pluck it out! But be careful you don't pull up the henbane."

Erwin reached his hand out for Anemone, but then Winnie nipped him in the leg. He screamed and began shrinking and shrinking and his voice grew lower and lower until there was nothing left of it but a delicate scritch-scratch. But no, that was not Erwin's voice at all. It was a bee whose legs were crawling over the anemone leaves with a tiny scrabbling sound. Or perhaps that was Aunt Gundula's pen scratching? No, it was nothing of the kind; it was Winnie's beard again. And it was Winnie's voice saying: "Anemone, he's wonderful!"

"Who is wonderful?" Anemone asked.

"Blue Boy, of course, Director Pampini's Clever Dog. Didn't you see the way he solved all kinds of hard arithmetic examples? Not because he can count, as some silly people think. What does a dog know about counting, or why should he want to know about it? But he understands every little gesture Director Pampini makes. That's more amazing than if he could count—why, the dullest school-boy can learn to do that. *I* think Blue Boy is the finest Kerry on earth. So smart, and so handsome besides. What a build he has, and that marvelous steel-blue color of his coat—my own famous silver-gray is drab by comparison. And his magnificent hindpaw! Did you notice how gallantly he allowed me to go ahead whenever we met at the entrance to the ring? And how elegantly he bent his head to sniff me today? And have you any idea what he said? Oh, you can't possibly guess. 'Lady Pooh,' he said, 'you are the star of stars. Beside you even Rosalie pales, not to speak of my own insignificant self. Too bad you're not a Kerry of good family! I must say your smell is as aristocratic as the best of Kerries, and your shape is true to the standard. But that color, my dear lady, that color!' And he turned away with a shudder. What am I going to do? I don't want to be a circus star; I only want to please you and him, the handsomest Kerry in the world. And that's impossible as long as I'm wearing this horrible coat of paint. Please wash it off!"

"But, Winnie darling, my sweetest, dearest doggie," Anemone said pleadingly—she had stopped being a flower and was a girl again—"have you forgotten that we are through with men for good, since Papa has been so unjust to us? Please, put any thoughts of Blue Boy out of your head. You can't fail me now. We have to provide for our aunts, and just selling Easter eggs won't do it. We need the two talers you make. Besides, if you didn't have your paint on you'd be recognized at once. You heard Erwin say that he's hired a whole gang of boys to hunt for us. Do you want them to find us and bring us back to horrid old Ilsebill? You'd be chained up for the rest of your life—and maybe she would even deliver you to the dogcatcher.

"No," Winnie replied sadly. "I certainly don't want that. And I'd sooner my heart would break than disappoint you. But the pork chops will be ashes in my mouth if I'm not allowed to tell Blue Boy that I am a true Kerry and a daughter of Skilligaly who wore the Great Star of the Crystal Palace on his collar."

"All right, you may do that. But he must be as silent as the grave."

"Thank you," Winnie said, and she licked Anemone's hand tenderly before jumping down from the bed and going back to her basket. "You can be sure Blue Boy will not betray us. He's a gentleman from his beard to the tip of his tail."

Anemone woke up for a moment and saw Aunt Gundula beside her, her pen still flying over the paper. In one of her black curls sat a bee, rocking as bees ordinarily do inside the chalice of a flower.

". . . and so I maintain with good reason that the cause of all the mischief is . . ." Aunt Gundula was writing, and then Anemone fell asleep again.

This time it was Minette who sprang onto the bed and purred gently into Anemone's ear. What was she saying? "Gardeners are supposed to be clearheaded people, aren't they? They're said to be able to hear the grass growing."

"Yes," Anemone said, "but what about it?"

"Your father," Minette purred. "He doesn't notice a thing. And yet a gardener of all people ought to call a spade a spade. Remember that, Anemone."

"Don't talk in riddles, Minette!" Anemone pleaded. "Everywhere you look there are riddles nowadays. It's beginning to get on my nerves."

"Remember the first full moon of spring," Minette went on, completely disregarding Anemone's plea. "Queer that human beings are so blind. And not only your father.

At the time of the spring full moon, day and night rest; dark and light are in balance. This is the time for action. The darkness sends out the Evil One, understand? The old legends tell all about him. Again and again he tries to conquer the world. Each time he has a different name, but he is always the same. Once he came as Genghis Khan—have you had him in school yet?"

"No," Anemone said. "Minette, I must say you're giving me shivers down my spine with all this mysterious business."

"He was a tyrant. Genghis Khan, I mean. The Wicked Owl was another one. Why are there less and less pretty pigeons on the cathedral towers? Nothing has happened to any of them here in the sexton's house—I see to that— and I watch our hens too. Spring is coming. But have you heard any finches calling this year? Or titmice twittering? Why isn't the blackbird singing its song in the linden tree by the cathedral, as it always used to in springs past? Why?"

"Why, why, why!" Anemone said impatiently. "That's what I would like to know."

"Call a spade a spade!" Minette purred. "Remember that, remember that."

"Call a spade a spade," Anemone repeated.

"What's the matter, my girl?" Aunt Gundula asked. "You keep talking in your sleep. I'll blow out the candle now. What was that you just said?"

"Call a spade a spade, Aunt Gundula. Minette said that to me, but what she means by it is beyond me. Ab-so-lu-tely!"

Marionettes

EVERY DAY a new batch of Easter eggs was decorated by the industrious ladies working in the small kitchen of Aunt Gundula's flat, or at the work table in the studio. Every day Anemone-Perdu took a basket of these beautiful eggs and sold them in the marketplace, and every day Winnie performed in Pampini's Circus and earned her two talers. The whole town of Vogelsang was talking about the clever little dog; people even came from the neighboring towns and villages to see this wonderful new performer—and at the same time made use of the occasion to buy a few of Gundula Immofila's famous eggs for their children.

The town's reputation, which had suffered a blow with the disappearance of the stone maiden and the ugly waterspout, was gradually coming back to normal. The Piebald Dog, as Winnie was called—Lady Pooh as she was known among the artists of the circus—made people forget, at

63

least for the time being, those deplorable events. She was the delight of grownups, the darling of the children, and the pet of all the circus performers. Signorina Bella, the blonde equestrian, refused to perform unless Winnie was sitting on her snow-white horse. Monsieur Renard, the Strong Man, stood in the ring sweating and grunting as he lifted dumbbells weighing hundreds of pounds. At the end of his number he would let Winnie drag away the biggest and heaviest of the weights—which would then prove to be hollow and made of cardboard. That brought down the house every time. The elephant Kim let Winnie ride on his back beside the Indian boy Ajunta, splendid in his white silk costume and huge turban. Anemone, too, was allowed to ride on Kim as often as she pleased. Very carefully and tenderly, almost like a devoted nurse handling a baby, he used to lift either Anemone or Winnie with his trunk and put them on his back.

Anemone had the time of her life at the circus. Never, she thought, had she met so many nice people all in one place. She loved having the free run of the caravans, of the stalls where the beautiful horses and ponies were kept, and of the big top. She chatted with the performers, played with the artists' children and with the animals and felt that they all looked upon her as though she were herself one of the troupe. Had it not been for the stab she felt in her heart everytime she thought of her father she would have been happy to go on like this for ever.

Often she sat with Director Pampini and his fat wife, Yolanda, in his caravan which was fixed up as the nicest little home on wheels imaginable. There was always Blue Boy around and a monkey or two. There was a parrot, called Ercole, who looked like a cousin of Lora and chattered happily from the back of the big couch, saying, 'Buon giorno, signorina! Buon giorno, ma bella. Oh carina madonna!" And Mrs. Pampini, who had once been a fine trapeze artist, chuckled delightedly. She was now plump and comfortable and had no artistic ambitions any longer. All she wanted was to make a nice home for her husband. Whenever Perdu dropped in she had saved a bone for Winnie and a steaming cup of hot chocolate was ready for the boy. In her funny way of speaking, liberally sprinkled with Italian words, she would tell stories of things and people she had seen on her many journeys all over the world. Or Mr. Pampini would talk about animals, which was for Perdu the most important and most interesting subject in the world.

"The main thing is, you never ask an animal to do what he does not like, what goes against his nature, see?" Mr. Pampini said. "Every animal likes to perform. You only must find out what he likes most, e presto! the rest is easy. Of course you can force an animal to do things by beating him and make him afraid, see? But no use! I would not have such terrified creatures in my circus. Not in the world famous Circus Pampini! Nonono!" And Director Pampini's black eyes flashed and his black mustache bristled with indignation and his wife beamed at him adoringly.

Sometimes Peeps and Ajunta took part in these cozy conversations, each one with a cup of hot chocolate before him, and they too treated Perdu as if he were a full-fledged member of the company and as if his opinion counted. That was a great honor, and Anemone was prouder of it than if she had got an A in French, which, by the way, did not happen very often.

The weather had turned colder again. A bitter wind was coming down from the mountains and it seemed almost as if there might be another snowstorm. At any rate it did not look like the beginning of spring, and the

town's oldest people who had experienced all kinds of
weather in their long lives, said that there had never been
a March like this one. And then they looked timidly
around to see that there were no eavesdroppers, and whispered that lots of things were happening these days that
they never had known to happen before.

From the beehive in Aunt Gundula's bedroom came
a low, mournful humming, and the pigeons in the gable
of the sexton's house didn't seem to want to fly out at
all. Most of the day they sat on their perches, feathers
puffed out disconsolately, and emerged only when Anemone came out to feed the chickens on the roof garden.
Even they stayed inside their coop most of the time. Only
the cathedral pigeons continued to circle above the square,
as though they no longer felt safe in their nooks and
crannies among the gothic stonework. Every so often the
dead body of a bird, its feathers sadly rumpled, would
be found lying on the pavement of the square.

"Haven't you heard anything new in the marketplace?" Aunt Gundula would ask every evening when
Anemone came home.

There was always plenty of news. "I see Erwin every
day," Anemone reported. "He keeps hanging around the
marketplace and poking into every corner. Sometimes
he's alone, sometimes he has half a dozen or more boys
with him. The nastiest boys in town are in his gang. All
the other children know he's after me, so they give me
a tip whenever they see him or old Schlummermutz coming. They don't know what it's all about, of course, but
they want me to sell my eggs in peace because I always
let them have a look into the basket."

"But why does Erwin keep after you? Has he recon-
gized you after all?"

"Nothing of the kind. It's because of the time I slapped

him and Winnie nipped him. Naturally he wants to pay me back. Maybe he does suspect there's something funny about me, too. Anyway he keeps trying to find out where I live. Whenever he and his gang see me they sneak along behind me, trailing me. But I go home a different way every day, and I always dodge them by slipping through a gate or down an alley and through back yards. While they're still standing and looking for me I'm back on Cathedral Hill and home. It's lots of fun."

"My goodness, you call that fun!" Aunt Lena moaned, covering her face and shuddering.

"If half a dozen of those hoodlums catch hold of one little girl you might find it a good deal less fun," Aunt Gundula said, shaking her head. "I'm beginning to see what a breathtaking business it is having an eleven-year-old daughter."

"Oh, they won't catch me," Anemone insisted airily. "You see I'm smarter than all seven of them put together."

"Confidence in yourself is a good thing," Aunt Gundula said. "But now come and tell us what else you've heard and seen."

"Everybody is saying that the marionette theater is marvelous. Tomorrow I mean to go while Winnie is busy with her act in the circus. The man who sits at the ticket window looks just like Uncle Eusebius. I'm going to ask him if he is."

"You seem to see Uncle Eusebius everywhere. First the figure on the egg and now the ticket-taker at the marionette theater. I assure you he would never do anything so useful and down-to-earth as selling tickets. But now don't get off the subject."

"That's what my teacher always says in school," Anemone said. "Let's see, what else was there? Oh, yes, people are saying the mayor is going to ban the sale of colored or painted hen's eggs for Easter. Because naturally if he's having all the eggs bought up, it makes him mad that there are still eggs around to be colored. The farm women are all worked up about it. He can't possibly forbid the sale of Easter eggs, can he, Aunt Gundula? They would have to pass a new law first, wouldn't they?"

"You have no idea the things a tyrant can do without bothering about laws and justice. That's just what makes him a tyrant. Anyhow it's good when you keep your ears open in the market as you have been doing so far, my dear."

"Do you mean to say our mayor is a genuine, regular tyrant?" Anemone asked, wide-eyed. "Like Genghis Khan and the Wicked Owl you have been talking about? Tell me more about them."

"Heavens, the questions the child asks!"

"Oh well, if you don't know it doesn't matter. I'll find out somehow. Because I would like to know what Minette meant . . ." But here she stopped, for it struck her as rather out of place to repeat to her aunts what a cat had said to her in her dream.

"The Wicked Owl," Tina said pensively, and after that she fell into silence and deep meditation.

"But what has that to do with Minette-the-Cat?" Lena asked. She had the kind of mind that wanted to penetrate everything. But she did not wait for an answer from Anemone. "The Wicked Owl was only a nickname, you know," she said. "I wish I could remember his real name. Aunt Gundula told you the other day that he made life miserable for the people of our town just the way the present mayor is doing. He's buried somewhere in the vaults of the cathedral."

"And a good, safe place for one like him," Anemone said. "I'll look him and Genghis Khan up in the encyclopedia tomorrow."

And that is what she did first thing the following day, looked up tyrants in the encyclopedia volume Tr to Ut. There seemed to have been quite a lot of them in history. But there was not a single word about the Wicked Owl in all the twelve volumes.

That day Anemone went down to the market very early so that she could dispose of her basketful of eggs and still be in time for the marionette show. After the eggs were gone she took Winnie over to the circus and had a chat with her friends there. Her pockets were stuffed, as they were every day, with tidbits for the circus animals—a fine bone for Blue Boy, an apple or carrot for Kim and Bijou. And there was always something for Rosalie, too. Pink and enormous, she lay in her caravan, her long ears dangling over her face, and whenever she was spoken to she replied softly, in the most refined French: "Oui, oui." Aside from food she was interested in nothing else but her fat, squirming, greedy babies.

"Make this a good one!" Anemone said to Winnie and Blue Boy, Bijou and Kim. But her reminder was not really needed, since the animals did their best at every show.

At the marionette theater Anemone bought a ticket for the lowest price seat—and took a good look at the ticket-taker. He had a heavy scarf wound around his neck and a cap pulled way down over his ears, and he was sniffing and snorting as though he had a frightful cold. His eyes were small and bloodshot and his nose swollen, but there could be no doubt who he was. "G'd evening, Uncle Eusebius," Perdu said.

The ticket-taker started as though he had been stung. He sneezed violently and snapped: "What do you mean by Uncle Eusebius, young fellow? Forget these silly jokes, I'm not your uncle. Here's your ticket. Kakakakakaka-choo!" And to the next in line, "Sorry, sir, sold out. No more seats for this performance."

As soon as Anemone settled down on the hard bench, the curtain rose, and for the next hour she forgot everything but the play.

When she came home in the evening there was a big casserole of Schinkennudeln on the table, and this being one of Anemone's favorite dishes she did not say much until she had eaten her fill. "If I could only cook like you, Aunt Gundula," she said after the last crumb had been cleared away. "Maybe I could have outcooked Ilsebill with her silly dumplings and made Papa forget about her."

"I can teach you to make dumplings, too," Gundula said. "But now tell us about the marionette show."

"It's some show, I tell you! Those marionettes are like real people. There was a tyrant in the play, isn't that strange? What I would like to know is: Why do tyrants tyran?"

"Tyrannize, darling!" Aunt Lena corrected her.

"All right, tyrannize. Why do they? They can't possibly enjoy everybody being afraid of them and hating them."

"This is one of the questions mankind had been puzzling about since the times of the cavemen," Tina said.

"They want power"—Gundula tried to make it clear—"and they pay the price for it. They renounce love and decency and truth and every sound, normal human relationship. They are absolutely alone, but they don't mind, if they only have power."

"If they did mind whether other people like them, they would not be what they are," Aunt Lena added.

"Oh my!" Anemone sighed. "It *is* rather a puzzle. And another funny thing is that they always want people to agree with them. In this show there were the three chamberlains of the princess who did not agree with the emperor and that's how all the trouble started. Imagine, smuggling his own daughter away and then saying her chamberlains had done it. Plain mean I call that."

"We would thank you to begin at the beginning," Aunt Gundula told her.

"Well that *is* the beginning. There was a Chinese emperor. His name was Tsin Shi, and they said he was the Son of the Sun. And then there was his daughter Lu Wi Seh, which means Crown of the Universe, they told us. Otherwise I would have thought it meant just Luise. My! You should have seen her. All a-glitter and a-glamor. Her dress embroidered with golden dragons and birds and things over and over. She was sitting on a smaller throne on the right side of her father's big throne, and on his left sat Mo Ko, his favorite lap-dog, who was constantly fanned by a sweet little slave girl. Now this princess, Lu Wi Seh, was spoiled. You should have heard the way she talked to the mandarins! And I'm sure that Lu Wi Seh never thought of washing a single dish in her life. All she did was sit on her throne and sneer at all the nice princes who had come to ask her to marry them. Why anybody would want to marry such a girl is beyond me. But her father loved her so much that whatever she did was all right with him. Some fathers are like that, but not all. She gave the poor princes such hard riddles to solve that nobody could possibly answer them. Then she told them to go to the Big Western Mountains and get for her the Three Jewels which the dragon Wu was keeping in his cave. Everybody knew that no mortal man could do such a thing, but when the princes hesitated she called them cowards and sent them away with their long pigtails cut off. And her father only smiled instead of spanking her.

"The most pitied men in the whole country were the
three chamberlains of the princess, three very noble lords.
Lord Yu was short and fat, Lord Ku was tall and thin,
and Lord Shu was just middle. They had to keep the
princess in good humor and they were responsible to the
emperor for her safety, which was an awful job, because
that girl was always up to tricks. One time when the
three lords were alone in the courtroom I could hear them
whisper that the emperor wanted to destroy them, that
was why he had given them this job. I didn't quite understand what it all meant, but that was what they said.

"In the second act there was a great commotion in the
palace; you could guess right away that something awful
must have happened. And it had. That Lu Wi Seh had
broken the yellow porcelain button on her father's morning cap and had scattered the broken pieces so that Mo
Ko cut his tender little paws. This was too much even
for her father, and all at once he turned against her and
talked to her almost in the same way as Papa talked to
me. He ordered her to go to her room and stay there
three days and nights. Only the emperor had the key to
her apartment and the three lords had to play checkers
with her. This was an awful thing for them because she
got mad when they won, and when they let her win she
said that they had not paid proper attention to the game.
But most of the time she was screaming and making a
big fuss and behaving abnormally—I mean abominably.
My, it made me wish that some people could see how
other people's daughters carry on!"

"No personal remarks, if you please!" Aunt Gundula
said.

"And then, what do you think happened? After three
days, when the emperor came with the key to let her out
again, she wasn't there any more. She had disappeared,

just melted away, nobody knew where!"

"Disappeared!" Lena cried out, glancing meaningly at Gundula and Tina.

"Absolutely," Anemone confirmed. "Vanished, you know. The emperor instead of being glad to be rid of her nearly had a fit with rage. It was all the chamberlains' fault, he said. They had spirited her away, they would be held responsible, of course, and when in seven days the princess was not found, they would be hanged and beheaded and quartered and I don't know what else. I was terribly scared for them, they being such nice men and absolutely innocent."

"How did you know they were innocent?" Aunt Lena asked.

"Well, practically everybody knew. I mean they were not the sort of men who would do such a thing. A woman who sat next to me said the same. 'They've never done it,' she said."

"Interesting," Tina said.

"And you should have seen the poor things search and search for the nasty girl, all in vain of course. At last they asked leave to go to the Big Western Mountains and see whether perhaps the dragon Wu had stolen the princess.

"I think that was exactly what the emperor had wanted, and the woman next to me thought so too. Because the emperor thought the dragon would kill the three lords which seemed the best way to get rid of them. 'You may go,' he said, 'but don't deceive yourselves. My arm can reach you even there. In seven days you must be back, or else . . . What I believe is that you have delivered her imperial highness the princess into the hands of our country's enemies.'"

"Tsk, tsk," Gundula said, and Anemone continued.

"When the curtain rose again there were mountains of rocks all over the stage, a waterfall was plunging down from high up and a black cave yawned like the open mouth of a giant beast.

"The three lords came up a narrow path looking so exhausted that I expected them every moment to drop dead. Which they did. At least two of them, Yu and Ku. Shu climbed on bravely until he reached the entrance of the cave. There was a hideous snorting coming from the cave, and sniffling and sneezing. It sounded like this man outside who looks like Uncle Eusebius.

"But really it was the dragon Wu who lived there, and what do you know, he was the most lovable character of the whole play. Shu was trembling with fear for he did not know that Wu was such a peaceful and nice animal. The poor dragon got quite excited when he heard that Shu suspected him of having stolen the princess. He would never dream of stealing a girl like her, he said. It was the Son of the Sun himself who had brought her up in a golden sedan chair carried by four slaves, and he had ordered the dragon to keep her until he came back for her. So that's what the emperor had gone and done, and then he pretended the poor lords had done it!"

"The emperor!" exclaimed the three aunts all together. "This monster of an emperor put her away himself and then he accused innocent people!"

"And on top of it all he had arranged with the princess that she should find out where the dragon was keeping the Three Jewels and try and get them. The dragon told Shu all about her. He said he could not stand it any longer. His health was suffering. He would have thrown her over the cliff, he said, if he had not been under the spell cast by Weng-the-Magician, which all the dragons in the middle kingdom had to obey. As long as they lived in the emperor's territory they had to obey his commands. The magician had no power over the Three Jewels though.

"'I'm worn out,' the dragon sobbed. 'I'm not fit for such a job. When I fell asleep at last from sheer exhaustion, she poured kerosene into my nostrils. I ask you, what would you expect to happen, considering the fiery character of my breath? Luckily there was only a small explosion, but I have never felt myself since. My poor nose is frightfully sore. Then yesterday she took the most beautiful scales off my back to make herself a pair of alligator slippers. But that was nothing compared with the language she used. If I ever had done that in my childhood my mother would have scrubbed my mouth with soap, I assure you. I couldn't listen to that language any longer.'

"That's about what the dragon said. Finally his patience had given out. He promised to show her the Three Jewels and lured her into the deepest chamber of the cave and rolled a heavy rock before the entrance. But he would have to feed her today, so what should he do? 'Couldn't you take her away, oh bravest and noblest of knights?' he pleaded. 'I promise I would leave the middle kingdom for ever and move to my cousin's in Tibet where there are no tyrants as far as I know.'

"Shu said he must think about it. 'And what are your terms, oh mighty dragon, revered elder brother?' he said. They seem to be extremely polite over there in China. 'Do you think we want to be saddled with the care of that infernal girl again?' Shu asked. 'I'm afraid such a favor will cost you something.'

"'With the greatest pleasure I'll give you the Three Jewels,' the dragon said. 'You can tell the emperor you have killed me and taken them away, and when you have them he must do everything you order him to. There is first the onyx ring which heals illness, revives the dead and discovers the truth.'

"When Shu heard that, he wanted first thing to bring his two friends to life again. He only touched them with the ring, and they woke up and were as good as new. The second treasure was a great piece of jade carved with the image of the Heavenly Dragon, the lord of all monsters and spirits, the sight of which makes tyrants powerless and explodes every deceit."

"Exposes, probably," Aunt Lena said.

"At any rate Shu said this jade might prove very useful. At last the dragon produced a wonderful glowing red ruby from the deepest bowels of the Western Mountains, he said. Did you ever know that mountains have bowels? This stone, he said, healed broken hearts and united split-up lovers.

"And now you should have seen Shu. He hopped around like mad and sang a little song saying that he had wished for this ruby many, many years, for the lady of his heart was cross with him because he had gone away without taking proper leave of her."

"Is that what they do in China?" Gundula asked.

"That's what Shu said. It was not so easy to understand what the dragon said, so I may have made some mistakes. He was weeping, sneezing and snorting so miserably all the time that it would have melted a heart of stone. And how happy he was to see the three lords leave with the princess. He hid behind a rock, of course, so that she would think the lords had killed them. But she was quite quiet anyhow because she was scared to death of the jade stone with the image of the Heavenly Dragon.

"In the last scene the three lords, bringing the princess with them, entered the courtroom of the imperial palace in great triumph. The emperor looked purple with rage that they had not only returned alive and as great heroes, but that they also had won the Three Jewels. When he saw the onyx ring he had to admit that he had taken the princess away himself to spite the three lords. And when they pushed the jade stone under his nose he trembled and tittered and could not do a single thing against this great charm. He only pleaded for mercy. The three lords had no intention of taking away his throne. It was not their intention to rule, they said, as in their opinion ruling other people very easily spoils one's character. Then they told old Tsin Shi that he must from now on rule with mildness and justice. He had to promise, cross his heart, to do no wrong any more, to relieve his people of all taxes and forced labor, and to put Lu Wi Seh into the convent of the Holy Tortoise until she should be a truly reformed character. And the lords warned the emperor if they ever should hear any complaints they would come down hard on him and by the power of the Heavenly Dragon banish him and his daughter from the middle kingdom. And you should have heard the people cheer and shout when the three lords took their leave and returned to their castles, Yu and Ku to their families, Shu to find his lady and see whether he could make up with her."

"It must have been a remarkable play," Lena said. "Tomorrow we'll go and see it, Tina, that's for sure."

"And in the end," Anemone said, "when the audience had cheered and clapped hands like mad the woman next to me said that something like the carved jade stone might be a handy thing to have around. Perhaps it might even help to find the vanished stone maiden of the cathedral, she said. All the people around roared with laughter, although Schlummermutz was standing at the entrance of the theater booth looking like black thunder."

• • •

Late that evening when they all were lying in the Dream Ship, Anemone began again to praise the marionettes and the clever people who had been playing them, especially the one who was doing the dragon Wu, because he sniffled and sneezed in the most natural way, and come to think of it, Anemone said, it could have only been the ticket-taker. "Such a darling dragon," she said sleepily. "Just the gentlest creature ever. I wanted so much to pet and comfort him. I couldn't help feeling terribly sorry about the kerosene in his poor nose."

Gundula did not do any writing this evening. She put her arm around Anemone, and Anemone cuddled up comfortably in the crook of her elbow. Everything was so cozy. The animals, too, were sleeping peacefully in their rose-colored basket. Now it did not matter so much that outside in the stormy March night the screech of the owl sounded from the cathedral towers. Anemone felt safe in the big bed, and she knew the nasty owl could not do any harm inside Aunt Gundula's room.

"What was it that Lord Shu said about the red ruby?" Gundula asked softly after a while.

"He said he could use it," Anemone answered dreamily. "He said the lady of his heart was mad at him for going away without taking proper leave or something of the sort."

"Oh," Aunt Gundula said, blowing out the candle.

A Bleak Day

ON WEDNESDAY OF Holy Week, when the Dream Ship once more docked on the shore of waking life, the three aunts got out of it with grave and thoughtful faces, as though they had had a stormy night's voyage. Only Anemone woke up gay and happy as a skylark. It was a wonderful life for her up here in the gable apartment of the old sexton's house. Never a dull moment, with the circus and the selling of the eggs which was quite dangerous by now, and being chased by Erwin and his gang and by fat old Schlummermutz, neither of whom would ever get her, she felt sure. And then there wére all the wonderful books on Gundula's shelves, and very little dusting and dishwashing to do, as Aunts Lena and Tina said that they needed some work to distract them from their sad thoughts. With Anemone it was completely the other way round. She only had sad thoughts when she was standing before a sink piled high with unwashed dishes which she was supposed to do.

She had another reason to be especially cheerful today. She had earned some extra money by cleaning up Kim's caravan and had used it in what she considered an extremely wise and reasonable way. She knew that her father would be completely reassured and at ease when he read his newspaper this morning at the breakfast table and found something in it which would end all his worries about his daughter.

"Did you hear the owl screeching during the night?" Aunt Lena asked over the coffee table, giving her shoulder a jerk as though a shudder were running down her spine. "Every hour that wretched bird screeched. I heard it right through my sleep."

"I didn't," Anemone said, biting into a crispy crescent bun. "I slept just wonderfully."

But Aunt Gundula nodded at what Aunt Lena had said. "No wonder. During Holy Week the church bells, which otherwise keep down the deadly creatures of the night, are silent. It's lucky we have Minette to guard the hens and the pigeons in the gable."

"Why don't the bells ring?" Anemone wanted to know.

"Don't you know that they fly away to Rome before Easter to get themselves blessed for the whole year?" Aunt Gundula said. "They come back in time for the resurrection service on Holy Saturday evening." Then she buried herself behind the morning paper and was lost to the world. She kept mumbling under her breath, she shook her head, and ignored the breakfast table conversation. But suddenly she looked up, stabbed her finger at a place in the paper, and eyed Anemone sharply.

"Oh, that," Anemone said. "I put that in to comfort him, you know."

And then Aunt Gundula read aloud:

"Attention! To Mr. Benjamin Florus. Have no fear for your daughter's safety, even though you may not see her again. She is all right and in good health. A friend."

"Is that what you call comforting?" Aunt Tina demanded.

"Isn't it? Now he knows I'm alive."

"True," Aunt Lena said, and added, "Poor man."

"And here, another juicy item," Aunt Gundula exclaimed, and laid the newspaper on the table, but she immediately picked it up again. "No, I'll read it aloud. This is really the height. Listen:

"'In our progressive age there are unfortunately still a good many persons who let themselves fall for outworn medieval superstitions. It must be said once and for all that for intelligent and clear-thinking people there can be not the slightest connection between the nightly cry of an owl from the cathedral towers and the regrettable disappearance of certain irreplaceable works of art. This must be stated publicly and loudly if our town is not to become the laughing-stock of the whole country. Men who have seen something of the world and have a broader horizon than the body of our fellow citizens . . .' and so on and so on. How do you like that, my dears?"

"Outrageous!" Aunt Tina exclaimed. "As though all of us were a bit off in the upper story."

"Seen something of the world—a broader horizon. And signed E. . . . Not very hard to identify, is it?" Aunt Lena said.

"To think he was once a friend," Aunt Gundula said, and became absorbed in the newspaper again. "The time is nearing," she murmured several times as she read. "The time is very close—that I can see clearly with my limited horizon. Tomorrow night the moon will be full— the Easter moon, the first full moon of spring." And suddenly she turned again to Anemone who had been listening attentively but had so far made no comment. "What was it you said the other day, I mean the other night, when you woke up, about calling a spade a spade? I keep thinking about that. It *is* important to call things by their right name. But what if one doesn't know the name!"

"That's what Minette said. Human beings were so blind that they never guessed the right names, she said. And she said something about the first full moon of spring also."

"If Minette has to tell somebody something I wonder why she doesn't tell it to me," Aunt Gundula said, somewhat offended. "Am I her mistress, or who is?" She looked sharply at the cat who was lying in her basket with an expression of complete innocence on her face. "You cunning thing!" Aunt Gundula said to Minette. "And maybe you are right. That old book by Nostradamus on the shelf..."

"Another tyrant?" Anemone asked interestedly.

"Don't interrupt, Anemone. It is considered very bad manners. This Nostradamus was one of the greatest magicians of the middle ages, if you must know. And he says that most evil spirits are obliged to return to their true forms when they are called by their proper names."

"That's what Minette must have meant!" Anemone exclaimed. "Calling a spade a spade."

"I too have something I must look up in a book," Aunt Lena said, nodding gravely. "Perhaps that'll help. If only I knew that Rafael wasn't home...."

"If you intend to look up the Wicked Owl," Anemone said, "I can tell you that he isn't in the books."

"Maybe he is in the book I have in mind," Lena said. Meanwhile Tina was looking out over the roofs of the town. "I am sure he hasn't a single pair of whole socks to wear." She sighed. "And what a state the house must be in!"

"If I were you," Anemone said, "I'd go home and darn a few socks." But no one seemed to pay attention to this sound advice.

"Do you happen to know, Gundula, where the keys of the vestry are kept? I mean the small one which is not in use any longer, where the statues were put for cleaning?" Aunt Lena asked.

"The sexton keeps the keys, of course," Aunt Gundula replied. "He has a whole cupboard where the big, hand-forged keys hang. The sexton's wife once showed it to me. It's a glass-fronted cupboard which is always kept locked. His wife said that the sexton guards the key to that cupboard so well that he keeps it under his pillow at night when he is sleeping."

"Oh, but the sexton's cupboard can't be anything compared to the big key cupboard in the Town Hall!" Anemone exclaimed. "Papa told me about that one. He said he never in his life saw so many keys in one place. The mayor we used to have, the nice one, showed them to him once. Keys to all the town buildings and the churches and I don't know what else."

"Really!" Aunt Gundula said. "I should have thought so. Well, we shall see. Tomorrow is the equinox and also the spring full moon. When those two events come together, all the forces of light are awake to fight the powers of darkness."

"It's about time to do something about those powers of darkness," Aunt Tina said. She was standing by the window, gazing out beyond the winding millstream toward the pointed gables of the street called Crooked Alley. "Right after Easter the High Criminal Court holds its session and our poor husbands go on trial."

This subject always made the aunts low-spirited, so Anemone was glad when Aunt Lena and Tina and even Aunt Gundula, who so seldom went out, put on their coats, one after the other, and marched down the stairs, each one on some mysterious errand of her own.

Anemone stayed home alone with the animals. She brought the pillows of the big bed out to the roof garden so that they could air, fed the three hens, scattering a few extra grains of corn for the pigeons. She washed the breakfast dishes because there was nobody else to do it today. But she didn't mind much for she had such a lot to think about. The animals trooped after her from one room to the other, and when the work was done they all played at Cat-and-Mouse for a while. Later Anemone went to Aunt Gundula's bookshelf, took out a book and settled down snugly in the big armchair by the window. It was a volume of Shakespeare, a play called *Richard the Third,* and this man, Shakespeare, seemed to know a thing or two about tyrants, too. A good author, Anemone thought, but even he did not say a word about the Wicked Owl. However, he kept her spellbound and the morning passed in a jiffy.

All at once, so it seemed to her, the clocks in the towers of the town struck twelve, but none of her aunts had returned. She spread some bread with honey for herself, fed Winnie, Minette, Lora and Snow White, took another good look at the beautiful Easter egg on the chest, and then gazed out of the window as her aunts had done this morning. Everything looked bleak and gray. The wind was sweeping over the square and through the streets, whirling dust into the air. Heavy clouds scudded across the sky like big, dark ships. It was hard to imagine that Easter, the feast of spring, was only a few days away.

How wonderful Easter had always been in the past, when Anemone's mother was still living. And even last year, when she had been alone with her father. On Holy Saturday evening they had gone, as they did every year, to the service in the cathedral. The choir had sung so solemnly: "Death, where is thy sting? Hell, where is thy victory?" The great *Te Deum* had swelled through the nave of the old church as though even the stone pillars were joining in the singing. Then the bells of the acolytes had tinkled and the big cathedral bells which had been silent all Holy Week had suddenly found their voices again. "Do you hear the Gloriosa?" Papa had whispered into Anemone's ear. High in the tower the Gloriosa, the huge, ancient, sacred bell, had clanged out its song. There was no other bell like it in the whole country. And Anemone had snuggled closer against her father and felt deep in her heart how much they belonged together and how safe and happy she was with him.

And this year? Would Ilsebill and Erwin be sitting with Papa in the Florus's family pew? Anemone had a burning feeling in the pit of her stomach when she thought of those two sitting next to her papa as though that were their right. There it was—now she, too, was feeling black, like everyone else.

There was still no sign of her three aunts. It was time for Anemone to put on her boy's clothes and become Perdu. She filled her egg basket, called Winnie and went down to the marketplace. When she delivered Winnie at the circus, she found even Peeps the clown in a bad humor. "Every day busybodies are coming to ask who Lady Pooh belongs to," he growled. "Especially a lady, with the ugliest brat of a boy I've ever seen, keeps after us about it. She says the dog bit her son and, if that's true, I am sure he deserved it. And yesterday we had a visit from the police—probably the lady got them on our necks. It seems some silly little girl has run away with her dog, or been kidnapped or something, and they seem to think we have something to do with it. I've told them a hundred times if I've told them once that the dog belongs to a boy, not a girl."

"Don't they believe you?" Perdu asked innocently.

Peeps waved his hand in a weary gesture. "You might just as well save your breath as argue with the police. Early this morning some policeman who looks like a walrus was here and had the director on the carpet. 'It is my duty to point out to you,' he said, 'that your, ah-hum, enterprise can be, ah-hum, shut down if there is any illegality in connection with that dog. Which is to say, if the public performances of said dog do not conform to police ordinances and the edicts of Higher Authority. Does the dog have a license?'"

"That was Schlummermutz!" Anemone exclaimed. "Our Chief Constable. Doesn't he spit through his teeth as he talks? Yes? Then that's him. Marvelous how you imitate him, Peeps. Don't let him get you down. Now I have some things I must do. So long."

"So long, Perdu. Life is a puzzle."

"I've been feeling that way myself today."

Now there were the eggs to sell. The basket was well covered so that the contents were concealed from those who had no business knowing. The foot of the Column of Justice was a good place—there was always a sizable crowd. "Easter eggs," Perdu whispered to passers-by. "Genuine Immofila eggs!"

That was like a magic spell. Everybody wanted an Immofila egg, all the more so because of the ban on the sale of eggs. Anemone's basket was soon empty. It was still early and her enemies, the gang of boys, had not yet appeared. But sure enough, there was Erwin, out walking with his mother! Anemone stole along behind them and tried to catch what they were saying. Perhaps I'll find out something about Papa, she was thinking.

"Tomorrow is the day, Erwin, tomorrow and no later," Ilsebill was saying, and she patted the boy's bristly hair. "Otherwise it's all up with us and our fine plan. Instead of sitting warm and cozy in a nice home, we'll be out in the cold and rain again. Be nice to Mr. Florus and quiet and obliging. And don't forget we have to find that Anemone."

"What am I supposed to do about that?" Erwin grumbled. "First you wanted to get her out of the house, and now that she and her nasty dog are gone I'm supposed to bring them back again."

"Yes, I know, I expected it to turn out differently. I thought that once she was out of the way we would have a free hand. But now it's just the opposite. You can't figure people out, that's all."

"For the last three days I've been trailing that boy who sells Easter eggs, the one who brings the funny-looking dog that bit me to the circus and comes to fetch it again. But he manages to get away every time as though the ground swallowed him. We haven't been able to find out where he lives."

"You *must* find out today, I tell you. That dog is Winnie or I'll eat my hat. And wherever Winnie is, Anemone must be nearby."

"Do you think I feel like being punched in the nose or having my leg bit again?" Erwin whined. "Tell your friend the mayor to put his policemen to work. I'm sick and tired of this whole business."

"The police!" Ilsebill exclaimed. "We'd have a long wait if it were up to them. Old Schlummermutz is good for nothing but twirling his mustaches. And if the first night of spring goes by, our game is up. Florus hangs his head like a weeping willow and hasn't so much as looked at me since the kid skipped out. And you know he has to kiss me and promise to marry me on the night of the spring full moon if our plan is to work. Anemone must be brought back, no matter how."

Again Erwin mumbled something, but what it was Anemone could not make out because the unpleasant pair had turned up the steps to the Town Hall and now disappeared through the great door. Anemone just caught Ilsebill's high-and-mighty words to the doorkeeper: "To the mayor's office!"

Lost in thought, Anemone returned to Cathedral Square. She noticed, coming down Market Street toward her, two men, one tall and gangling, the other short and stocky. The tall man was not saying much, but he kept shaking his head sadly as though in despair over the wickedness of the world. The fat man was wearing a soft hat and strong eyeglasses, through which he stared dismally at the pavement as he kept up an uninterrupted flow of talk. It was not hard to recognize the two as Uncles Agamemnon Winkelriss and Rafael Trippstrill.

"Sick!" Uncle Agamemnon lamented. "He says he's sick in bed, the wretch. Letting a common cold lay him flat like that. Who's going to pinch-hit for the Dragon now? It was the sneezing and snuffling that made the success of the part, I tell you. That cold was Heaven-sent. But now he tells us he's on his deathbed. It's an outrage, it's just a tragedy, Rafael. For Heaven's sake, man, say something—you'll drive me crazy with your silence."

Uncle Rafael smiled wearily. "What is there to say, Agamemnon?"

"Be quiet! Everything was going so beautifully. Another three days of a full house and we would have been able to pay our rent, have a month's living in advance and buy a little something for our wives besides. And Eusebius has to go and have a breakdown."

"It's no use anyhow. What's the good of buying presents when we don't even know where our wives are."

"Don't talk so much, Rafael, you're giving me a headache. Haven't I been saying all along that there's just no sense to it any more? And now on top of all the police are making trouble for the marionette theater. Schlummermutz is talking about improper jokes and scoffing at authority and wants to see the license. If the mayor finds out that *we* are the players, good night!"

Uncle Rafael nodded: "Still, it's a good sign that the mayor feels our play has hit home. Seems to prove that he must have spirited the statue away himself in order to get us in trouble. If I only knew how anyone can make a heavy stone statue disappear so easily. It took a whole crew of men to move the thing to the vestry. That is what has been puzzling me all along."

"There's something not natural about it, I tell you, even if Eusebius sneers at us and calls it all medieval superstition. To tell the truth, I think he takes that line only to contradict Gundula Immofila. The two of them are like dog and cat. Oh, if only we had listened to our wives when they advised us to steer clear of the cathedral statues. But now it's too late."

Whereupon the two turned in at the door of Uncle Eusebius's crooked old house. Anemone sauntered off jauntily and full of good spirits, thinking: Won't I have things to tell the aunts when I get home. She did not yet suspect how much more was going to happen before she got home.

• • •

"Thank God you're here at last!" all three aunts exclaimed with one voice when Anemone at last reached Aunt Gundula's attic apartment just as twilight was settling over the roofs of the town. "But what a sight you are! What has happened? Where is Winnie?"

"I wasn't able to go back for Winnie," Anemone said, panting and in so weak a voice that her aunts grew even more alarmed. "You see, they almost caught me this time. I had to keep on the hop, so I thought I'd better leave Winnie at the circus with her friend Blue Boy until tomorrow."

Anemone looked like a soldier who had just come out of battle. A handkerchief of very questionable cleanliness was wrapped around her knee, and from her close-cropped blonde hair a thin rivulet of blood trickled down on her cheek.

"No need for excitement," she said, for in spite of her wounds and weariness she was obviously pleased with her part in the day's events. "If I hadn't slipped into the cellar I would have been home an hour ago. I'm starving."

One of her aunts ran into the kitchen for Anemone's supper, which they had been keeping warm for her. Another fetched the bottle of iodine for swabbing on her cuts, but the joint decision was to let the child have her supper first. And after Anemone had cleaned her plate with what appeared to be a healthy appetite, they could no longer contain their curiosity. "Now, please, tell us what happened and stop keeping us on tenterhooks. We were frightfully worried about you."

"The whole police force was up and about," Anemone began, quite smug' about being the cause of so much fuss. "As I was walking along among the booths in the market I heard Schlummermutz say to one of his men

that today they had to nab that boy with the piebald dog
and bring him to the Town Hall—the mayor had issued
strict orders. I thought: Wait and whistle, mister, you
won't catch me. Then, just as I went to get Winnie after
the afternoon performance one of Erwin's gang, who was
standing watch, saw me and started shouting. And now
the chase was on. They ran after me all through the old
part of town, but since I know every alley and gateway,
I gave them the slip. I scooted through some backyards
and up some stairs, came out again at the bridge, across
the Flea Market and down Faust Street, and before they
could say boo I was up the cathedral steps. I was just
going to turn the corner when I saw Erwin standing there
and I almost ran straight into his arms. Luckily he was
looking the other way, but I couldn't head for home, and
so I squeezed into a corner of the cathedral, between two
pillars with Moses and another old gent, and all of a
sudden . . ."

"What all of a sudden? Do go on."

"Let me catch my breath. Well, all of a sudden the
floor gave way under my feet. I slid and slid and slid
down something. It was a narrow little staircase, I found
out later. When my head stopped ringing, because I'd
bumped it quite a bit, there I was sitting right in the
middle of a lot of stone coffins."

Lena clapped her hand to her face. "You poor child.
How horrible!"

"Why horrible? I've always wanted to see a real vault.
Nothing but coffins, I tell you. All made of stone. And
one of them was open. So I looked in, but there was
nobody in it. The lid lay on the ground beside it. . . ."

"What was on that lid?" Gundula asked tensely. "Were
you able to see much down there? Tell me, was there a
figure of a man with a sword carved on the lid, and above
his head a big bird?"

"Let me see. At first it seemed rather dark, but after a while I could see pretty well. Some light came from the top of the stairs. That's right, there *was* a man with a sword on the lid, and I thought it was a parrot on his shoulder, but it could've been an owl too. And there were letters, but kind of worn and faded."

"Do try to remember, Anemone," Aunt Gundula said, giving Anemone's shoulder a little shake in her urgency. "What did they say, those letters?"

Anemone shut her eyes and pressed her lips together in a great effort to visualize. At last she said slowly, "There was first something and then O-W-N and some more. On top of its being so faded it was such an old-fashioned way of writing, you know. Wait a moment. Maybe it was O-W-L? Oh yes, I am pretty sure now. And could the first have been C-A-R-L, I wonder. Yes, CARL it was. CARL OWL," and then—she began to draw letters with her finger in the air, shaking her head, trying again. "CARL OWL OF OWLHILL?" All at once she was wildly excited, and so were her aunts. "Now I can see it quite clearly. CARL OWL OF OWLHILL! Do you think that's it? The name Minette had in mind and which is not in the encyclopedia and not in Shakespeare either?"

"Yes, yes!" Aunt Tina cried, but Aunt Lena cut in with, "No, no! Not Carl of course, and not hill, EARL OWL OF OWLHALL it must . . ."

And here Aunt Gundula interrupted her, not minding bad manners. "Are you quite certain there was a man-of-arms on the lid? And that the coffin was empty?"

"Absolutely," Anemone said. "A knight you might call him. And nobody in the coffin. I looked carefully, because I've always wanted to see a real-life skeleton, not just a plaster one as in the anatomy room in school. But no skeleton, nothing doing. So after a while I squeezed back up the little narrow staircase—and here I am."

"Thank heavens you are safely here!" Aunt Lena and Tina said and started to attend to Anemone's bruises.

Aunt Gundula went over to the bookcase, reached down a fat volume and lost herself in its pages.

"Ouch!" Anemone said. "That's enough iodine, Aunt Tina—it burns something awful. And now *you* tell me something. Did you go to the marionette theater today? I know for certain now that the man at the ticket window was Uncle Eusebius."

"There you're mistaken," Aunt Lena said firmly. "The man at the window today was a complete stranger."

"I said *was*," Anemone protested. "It couldn't have been him today because he's very sick. Maybe he's even dead by now. This morning Uncle Rafael and Uncle Agamemnon went to see him. I walked along in back of them and heard what they were saying. Uncle Eusebius sent word that he was lying on his deathbed with a frightful cold, and they were very sad and said what a pity because he had such a nice cold and who's going to speak the part of the Dragon Wu now."

"You see, Lena!" Aunt Tina cried. "You see, they are the marionette players. Didn't I tell you right off. I recognized the Emperor's voice."

"Of course they are," Aunt Lena replied. "If we weren't so blind and stubborn we would have realized it right away, when Anemone told us the story of the vanished princess. The dear men! So that was their secret. They wanted to make a little money, and we thought heaven only knows what they were up to behind our backs. Thank you for your hospitality, Gundula dear, I'm going back to my Rafael."

"And I to Agamemnon!" Aunt Tina said, bursting into tears.

"No, no," Anemone said. "You may just as well stay here. This evening when I passed the marionette theater it was closed and people were saying that Schlummer-mutz arrested the players after the afternoon performance and took them to jail."

"Oh, dreadful!" Aunts Lena and Tina groaned. Overcome as they were by their own troubles, they did not notice that Gundula had been growing paler and paler ever since Anemone had said that about Eusebius lying on his deathbed. But her habit of self-control came to her aid. *She* had no time to think about her own feelings.

"Let us be calm, my dears," she said, "and not do anything in haste. For today and tomorrow I don't want you to go. So much is going to happen you'll be better off here with me. Go on, Anemone. You look as though you have still more to tell us."

"Ilsebill went to Town Hall with Erwin because they have to find me, she said, because Papa is a weeping willow and doesn't even look at her any more. That's why the mayor, who's awfully thick with her, by the way, set the police after me. Because if I'm not found, she said, Papa won't marry her, but I don't think he'll do that anyway, and she doesn't want to have to stand out in the cold and rain, she said."

"In the cold and rain! Aha. And the mayor's thick with her . . . And the stone coffin was empty . . ."

"Yes, and she also said that Papa has to give her a kiss and that it has to be on the night of the full moon. Can you imagine *anyone* wanting to kiss Ilsebill?"

"So I thought!" Aunt Gundula interrupted, shutting her book with a bang. "The night of the full moon. We still have twenty-four hours; then everything will be decided all at once. Not only what becomes of Ilsebill, but the fate of your men and of our dear old town. For now I know that everything hangs together, which is just what I've always suspected. Know-it-alls with their remarks about medieval superstitions are going to learn a thing or two. They don't realize that anything can happen in Vogelsang. We are not just any dull ordinary town, we are . . ." There was a long pause before she said: "You've done very well, Anemone. I'm pleased with you."

Anemone beamed, and Aunt Gundula turned to Aunt Lena. "Now think hard," she said to her. "Try to remember exactly—just what took place that time three hundred years ago when the stone maiden disappeared?"

"That is why I went home today," Lena said eagerly. "I mean, of course, I wanted to look to the house and darn up a few pairs of socks. But I couldn't stop thinking about the Foolish Virgin and the Wicked Owl. And so I looked into that old leather-bound book which gives an account of the terrible uprising in our town. Finally I found the passage I had been trying to remember all this while. This is the story: the stone maiden wants to have a soul, and the only way for her to win one is if some man loves her and takes her for his wife. Her only chance for that to happen is when the first full moon of spring falls exactly on March twenty-first, when spring begins, and on Good Friday night, just as it does this year and did three hundred years ago. At that time Vogelsang was ruled over by Earl Owl of Owlhall; *that* was the name I tried so hard to remember. He made life miserable for all the poor folks of the town, and he wanted to marry the stone maiden because one heart of stone calls to another. But then came the great uprising and he was killed and buried in the deep vault. And of course, being dead, he couldn't marry her, so that was the end of her hopes.

"But there was something else in the book. Someone found the henbane and used it to lure her back into her niche at the cathedral, where she instantly turned to stone again. Now tell me, where is anyone going to find henbane in March?"

"Where, you ask? Perhaps in a greenhouse!" Aunt Gundula exclaimed. She jumped to her feet and began pacing about the room, her blue eyes flashing and her black hair crackling. "How lucky we have an expert on local history in our house, and a child who tumbles into cellars. Now at last it is all clear to me. To bed, to bed with all of you. I have a great deal still to do today, and Anemone's eyes are already falling shut."

"But there's something else I still have to say," Anemone piped up. "Old Schlummermutz came to the circus and said Lady Pooh is under suspicion. And, oh, yes, selling Easter eggs is absolutely forbidden—it's a new law and they'll announce it in the Market Square first thing tomorrow morning. And Augusta, the egg woman, she told me that tomorrow every single egg has to be turned in, and all the birds in town as well, no matter whether they're hens or pigeons or even canary birds, imagine that. Frieda, the pretzel seller, told her, and she heard it from somebody who's married to a cousin of Mrs. Schlummermutz. Only nobody is supposed to say anything about that yet, she said."

"Good," Aunt Gundula said. "Then it's open war you want, Mr. Mayor. So much the better. Now we shall see who is stronger, the powers of darkness, or we."

After Aunts Lena and Tina had taken themselves off to bed along with Anemone—the two aunts heaving heavy sighs over their poor husbands in jail, Aunt Gundula wrapped herself in her bright-colored dressing-gown and sat down in the flowered easy chair. She coaxed Lora over to the arm of the chair, called Snow White and Minette to her lap, and had a long conversation with them. That is, she talked and the clever beasts listened attentively.

The Battle of the Easter Eggs

HOLY THURSDAY MORNING, when Chief Constable Schlummermutz had been ringing his hand-bell and reading the new ordinance at each of the four corners of Market Square, the foot of Cathedral Hill and in front of the Town Hall, it became clear that the time had come when our good old town of Vogelsang had swallowed about all it was going to swallow. No sooner had Schlummermutz retired to The Merry Finch to refresh himself with a mug of beer after straining his voice, than the town started to hum and boom like a startled swarm of bees. Vogelsangers had taken a good many queer doings and much shady business good-humoredly, without seeming to mind too much. But this last order of the mayor's was the straw that broke the camel's back. What was this about there being no eggs at all for Easter? How were people to prepare their fried eggs with spinach for Holy Thursday, a dish which had been eaten on that day

from time immemorial? How were the good wives of the
town to bake their Easter cakes—for what kind of cake
could be made without eggs? But the most terrible part
of it was that all birds and fowl had to be turned in—
even harmless canary birds! It was said that the mayor
and his cronies loved such small birds in pies, and everybody whispered that on Easter Sunday there was to be a
great banquet in the Town Hall, at which a monstrous
fowl pie would be the main course. That was why the
town authorities had posted hunters armed with nets and
snares on all the hills surrounding the town to catch the
swarms of songbirds which were expected back any day
now. To think that this kind of thing could happen in
Vogelsang, the town that was so proud of having its
gardens and woods ringing all summer with the sweet
music of feathered singers!

Early in the morning of this eventful day, Gundula
Immofila, in her flat high above the roofs of the town,
told her friends to start baking Easter cakes.

What? Easter cakes? Hadn't she heard Chief Constable Schlummermutz's announcement only half an hour
ago?

She had heard. So what? Perhaps she thought that
Aunts Lena and Tina needed something to take their
minds off the subject of their jailed husbands. Then again
perhaps she meant to show that she, Gundula Immofila,
did not give a hang for the mayor and all his ordinances.
She had always been a law-abiding citizen, but there
were times when you had to disobey the law to keep
your own self-respect.

"Cake! Easter cake!" Aunt Lena exclaimed. "And what
are we supposed to say if Schlummermutz should come
up here and try to take the eggs out of your hencoop?"

"And who feels like eating Easter cake when our poor

husbands are languishing in prison?" Aunt Tina asked.

"Who says they will still be languishing there on Easter Sunday?" Aunt Gundula countered. "We must act as if everything were in order, and then everything *will* be in order. Holy Thursday is the time for baking Easter cakes. Our mothers and grandmothers and great-grandmothers did so before us, and nobody is going to stop us from doing likewise."

Aunt Lena dabbed her eyes with her handkerchief. "I don't feel much in an Eastery mood," she said. "And listen to that storm howling outside."

"Do you think I feel very Eastery," Anemone began whimpering, "when maybe Papa is giving that awful Ilsebill a kiss this very moment?"

"Now stop all this moaning and groaning!" Aunt Gundula snapped. "Get to work—that is the best medicine for sorrow. Leave all the rest to me, if you please." But then she glanced thoughtfully at Anemone. "Whatever are we going to do with you all day? Maybe I should lock you in or tie you up so that you won't get into trouble again. You've had enough bumps to last you for a year."

"I might go out looking for some henbane," Anemone offered modestly. "And I have to visit Winnie at the circus or she'll think I've forgotten about her. Once I have the henbane I'll look for the stone maiden and lure her back to her niche."

"Bright, aren't you? And do you have any idea where she is? Now you listen to me—don't you dare to leave the house today. Understand?"

"But this is tyranny!" Anemone cried out in alarm. "All of a sudden you turn tyrant, Aunt Gundula. It must be catching. And Winnie and I are all ag..."

"I *know!*" Gundula said, "and I would thank you to

keep you opinions to yourself for once." When she looked
as she did now, anybody would have known better than
to utter another word. And so did Anemone.

Meanwhile Aunts Lena and Tina had tied on white
aprons. Lena was already attending to a big bowl of egg
yolks, stirring as though her life were at stake. Tina sifted
the flour and set the yeast to rise in warm milk. Then
she cut strips of candied lemon-peel and rinsed the raisins. "You can shell more almonds, Anemone," she said.
With an offended look Anemone went ahead and shelled
the almonds, but her manner made it quite clear that she
was not enjoying her task.

"When the circus leaves town, Mr. Pampini is going
to take me and Winnie with him," she said sulkily. "Then
I won't have to go to school or anything and nobody is
going to be locking me in."

Aunt Gundula shook a threatening finger at her and
then left the kitchen to the crew of bakers. As she had
imagined, Aunts Lena and Tina soon became so absorbed
in their work that they forgot their sorrows for a while.
Anemone brooded darkly about her sad fate as she popped
one almond after the other out of its golden shell.

Gundula gathered Minette, Lora and Snow White
around her again. While spring rainstorm thrashed
against the windows and beat down on the square with
terrible force, the three in the kitchen heard Gundula's
voice speaking in measured accents in the other room.
They could not make out the words she was saying, but
she seemed to be repeating certain phrases over and over
again. At intervals Lora could be heard croaking back
what was being said to her.

Hours passed. The cakes had risen for the second time
and were ranged on the warming shelf ready to be popped
into the oven. Anemone had curled up in a corner with

a book. Now that the cake-making was over Aunt Lena began to be restless again. "I get so nervous, waiting for something to happen," she complained. "When I think of our poor husbands sitting in that cold, damp cellar, with Rafael so rheumatic anyway. And Gundula just plays with her animals as if there weren't a thing wrong."

"Gundula is not one to play at such a moment," Aunt Tina reminded her. "I am sure she knows a great deal more than she is telling us. Haven't you noticed that she's gone out more in the past few days than she usually does in a whole month? Trust her."

Afternoon came.

Up from Cathedral Square there rose the excited hum of many voices, like muffled thunder. Aunts Lena and Tina had long since taken the beautiful cakes out of the oven, glazed them with butter and dusted them with powdered sugar. Now the cakes were standing in a handsome row on the kitchen shelf, sending forth a heartwarming fragrance—raisin twists and almond wreaths and cinnamon-crumb cakes. But no one seemed able to take any real pleasure in them.

At last Aunt Gundula arose from her chair by the window, fetched her coat and galoshes, donned the high lambskin cap she had inherited from her mother, opened the bedroom door and made a soft, half-whistling, half-humming sound: "Tee-tay-tay-tee-tee-tum." Anemone and her two aunts stared in amazement, but any remark from them was clearly uncalled for. Aunts Lena and Tina threw each other a questioning glance. There came a tumultuous buzz from the beehive above the bed. The sound swelled and swelled until it was impossible to say whether it was the hum of the bees or Aunt Gundula's strange singsong—or was it the noise of confused voices from Cathedral Square below?

More and more bees came out of the hive and hovered like a golden cloud above Aunt Gundula's head. Gradually the humming died as one bee after the other settled in the wooly curls of the lambskin cap until at last the entire swarm was hanging in a giant cluster around Aunt Gundula's head.

"Good-bye," she said to the three who were still standing spellbound. "Good-bye, and help me with your wishes. Now I will discover whether I have figured everything out right or whether my reasoning is just outworn medieval superstition, as somebody called it. You will see me return victorious or not at all."

"And I'm supposed to stay at home!" Anemone wailed. "Just when at last something's going to happen!"

Accompanied by Minette, Aunt Gundula left the flat. Lora perched on her shoulder, and Snow White's pink nose peeped out of her coat pocket.

When the assembled populace of Vogelsang saw her coming down the steps of Cathedral Hill, surrounded by her swarm of humming bees, a great sigh of relief seemed to pass through the crowd. "Here she is!" they called out. "Gundula Immofila is coming. At last she's here!" And they rushed up to her, wailing and railing: "Have you heard the news? Winkelriss and Trippstrill are in jail! The circus and the marionette theater are closed! No fried eggs with spinach! No Easter cakes! Our birds must be turned in. And hunters are combing the woods with their nets!"

The crowd around Gundula consisted mostly of women. But more and more men, with righteous anger written on their faces, were joining in.

"Follow me!" Gundula said. "If you have the pluck to defend your rights, follow me to the Town Hall."

First, however, she asked the crowd to wait while she took a quick run over to the circus grounds. She found the director in his caravan, dully brooding over his predicament. Winnie and Blue Boy lay stretched at his feet, and seemed to bask in the bliss of being together. But Winnie sprang to her feet to greet Gundula—who saw that her sugar-coated beard was badly in need of a freshening up.

"I have come in place of Perdu, Mr. Pampini," Gundula said. "Don't lose heart. I hope you will be able to open up again on Saturday, and I am sure people will come to your circus by the thousands. But today I need your help."

The director declared himself ready to help any friend of Perdu's and Lady Pooh's, so Gundula briefly outlined her plan. Then, from her capacious handbag, she took out paints and brushes and a jar of fresh sugar-icing. She asked for several bowls of water. First she renewed Winnie's make-up and beard. Then she set to work on Blue Boy, who, at a word from his master, let Gundula transform him into an exact double of Winnie. When she was finished two piebald dogs stood face to face, wagging their tails as they regarded one another.

Gundula took them aside for a serious talk. She lifted her finger, pointed and rolled her eyes. And the two clever dogs listened attentively. "Do your part well!" she said at last, and gave each of them a parting caress. "And run for all you're worth. Now you, Mr. Pampini, will send Kim just as soon as Minette brings you word."

That arranged, Gundula returned to the waiting crowd, and led them toward the Town Hall. She strode along with head held high and bees buzzing in and around her fur cap. From every window along the way people watched, and from every door fresh forces poured to join her army. The farm women who sold eggs in the market were in the van. They were joined by the pastry bakers and the infuriated housewives who would be unable to serve their families with fried eggs and spinach—an omission unheard of in the history of Vogelsang. There were the mothers who wanted to give their children Easter eggs. Finally there was a long line of spinsters and old women, who carried their canaries and parrots in cages. They were shrieking and talking in great excitement, whereas the men moved in silence at their sides, armed with all sorts of tools. A blacksmith was hefting a mighty hammer; a carpenter had brought his saw, and several gardeners carried manure forks. They looked grim, determined and not easily intimidated.

The cries grew more and more threatening. "Eggs and spinach!" a frail little woman cried out at the top of her voice. "Liberty forever!" someone else shouted. Where had he come from, anyway, this new mayor who was acting so highhanded? Imprisoning honest men without trial! Ha! All eggs to the people! Protect the songbirds! Freedom of opinion for every citizen! Every person free to eat as many eggs and keep all the hens, pigeons and canaries he wanted. That was the way it had always been in Vogelsang, and that was the way they wanted it to stay.

When the crowd reached the Town Hall, they found the heavy doors barred and bolted. Their rage rose to terrible heights. "Open up!" they shouted. "We want to see the mayor!"

The doors remained shut. But after a while, as the volume of noise grew to ever more alarming proportions, the mayor appeared upon the balcony, importantly dressed in his purple robe, with the golden chain of office around his neck.

As soon as the tumult had died down a bit so that he could be heard, he addressed the crowd:

"Is that what you consider civilized conduct, my good people, to try and mob the Town Hall and threaten your mayor. You listen to agitators whose one desire is to stir up civil discord; you give way to indignation without knowing the facts or understanding the issues involved. Rest assured that your Town Council is working always for the good of the community. *We* know the facts and how to handle them. The budget is unbalanced; the treasury needs money. If we sell Vogelsang's great wealth in eggs to neighboring towns instead of selfishly and short-sightedly consuming them at home, every taxpayer will benefit. What is more, the songbirds, of which the town has made a cult these many decades, are by no means an economic asset. They rob the orchards and steal the grain while still in the fields."

In a firm, ringing voice Gundula Immofila replied: "Sir, you have much to learn about the habits of birds! Most songbirds feed on harmful insects. Considering the useful work they do in this regard, we can well afford to let them have the few berries and the scatterings of grain they take from time to time."

The crowd murmured approval, but the mayor chose not to hear Gundula's remarks. He continued: "As for the exaggerated number of canaries, parrots and parakeets kept in the town, these are so many useless mouths to feed. We have more serious problems to consider, my good people, and cannot waste more time on protest demonstrations over canaries. Enough of such nonsense, I say. Disperse peacefully. Return to your homes and your shops. Anyone who attempts to prolong this foolish insurrection will be considered an anti-social element and be treated as such."

"What kind of an ailment?" a man's deep voice cried out. "Ailment yourself! Why have you had Winkelriss and Trippstrill locked up without trial? Set them free!"

A woman's voice spoke up shrilly: "Sell our eggs to foreign towns? What you really mean to do is to eat them yourselves! Slaughter our hens and pigeons, exterminate and drive away our songbirds! Don't think you can make fools of us. We've kept quiet long enough. Our patience has come to an end."

"This is mutiny," the mayor cried, and he turned to consult with his councilors who were in a huddle behind the open door of the balcony. Once more he stepped out and shouted down into the square, in such a temper that he croaked hoarsely: "Go along home! Clear the square or I'll order the police to fire!"

That was something no one had expected. Fire upon the citizens of Vogelsang! Impossible!

But then Gundula spoke up calmly once more: "Do not do anything of the kind, your honor. Free the prisoners and then we will discuss other matters."

"I do not deal with agitators or their mobs," the mayor shouted. "Powder and lead is what you deserve, powder and lead is what you'll get. Free the prisoners! They are traitors, they belong on the gallows. If the square is not cleared in two minutes my men will shoot, shoot, shoot..." His voice broke with anger, and back of him in the conference room the councilors could be heard calling for Schlummermutz. But where was he? Where were the police of Vogelsang? Not a constable was in sight.

What had happened to Schlummermutz and his police force was this.

The two dogs, Blue Boy and Winnie, now looking like twins, had left the circus tent by two different exits.

Schlummermutz was lying in wait, and as soon as he caught sight of a dog he alerted his police and Erwin's gang of boys. Good old Schlummermutz wasn't too bright by nature, and by now he probably was more than a little confused. After all, the fruitless days of chasing a mysterious boy and his dog would have unnerved a better man than the Chief Constable. Just by the way and for the sake of historical accuracy it should be noted that Schlummermutz was not a real Vogelsanger. His mother had married into the town, and it was said that even on his father's side the family had been settled in our town for not even a hundred years. What can you expect of such a man?

At any rate, as soon as he set eyes on the dog, Schlummermutz shouted at the top of his voice: "There he is, the piebald dog! This time we'll catch him for sure!" He had not even noticed the rising excitement in the streets and the shouts of the people. It never entered his head that the police might be needed elsewhere. His wasn't the kind of head that can think of two things at the same time. And so he ran behind Winnie (or was it Blue Boy?) as fast as his short legs and still shorter breath allowed him to.

"The piebald dog!" The cry echoed from all sides. And from behind booths, from the cathedral steps, from the corners of streets and alleys, the pursuers came rushing. A wild chase began. In the excitement it passed unremarked that the swarm of policemen and boys split up at once—it never occurred to anyone that they might be chasing not one but two dogs. And so the group behind Winnie found itself heading out of town by way of St. Michael's Mount and the river meadows; the other group went tearing through the Old Town, out through St. John's Gate and deep into the municipal woods. Again and again the piebald dog appeared right before their eyes, almost within reach of their clutching hands. Again and again they thought they would have it in a moment, but it always put on an extra burst of speed and escaped them. All the while the dogs kept moving steadily away from town. And so it is not surprising that the entire constabulary force, consisting of Chief Schlummermutz and ten men, knew nothing at all of the disturbances in Town Hall Square.

Meanwhile Gundula had mounted the ledge of the fountain opposite the balcony. Now she gave a sign to Minette, and the lithe cat slipped quickly away. Silently, the crowd stood waiting, so tense that scarcely a breath could be heard.

And then, lumbering at a dog-trot down Market Street from the direction of Cathedral Square, came mighty Kim, the elephant, trunk raised high and uttering weird, raucous trumpet-calls, with Ajunta swaying on his back. The mayor had stepped back into the conference room.

"Break open the door, Kim, please!" Gundula ordered. The elephant lowered his iron-hard forehead. There was a brief groan of splintering wood, and the double doors flew wide open.

Gundula jumped down from the fountain ledge and beckoned the blacksmith to follow her. They entered the Town Hall and descended the steps to the cellar where the town lock-up was located. It was a small room with barred windows—prisoners are pretty rare in Vogelsang. With one blow of his hammer the sturdy smith broke the lock on the cell. And there stood Winkelriss and Trippstrill, gaping in astonishment at their liberators. "Come along," Gundula said curtly.

They went on up to the conference room in which the mayor and his councilors had meanwhile barricaded themselves. "Where is this confounded Schlummer-mutz?" one of the men behind the door could be heard complaining. Once more the smith used his hammer, and the councilroom door flew open.

Inside, the councilors had gathered around the mayor. The crowd of citizens had rushed up the stairs after Gundula and now thronged into the room.

"Mr. Mayor!" Gundula began. But the mayor, who had retreated to his seat behind the big conference table as if it were a fortress, would not let her speak.

"I know you! Beware. You will pay dearly for this. You are the one who is behind this whole rebellion. Your nasty animals attacked our constable when he was making an investigation of your premises. You have attempted to ridicule the government and incite people to evade its laws. And now open revolt! Seize her! Schlummermutz! This creature is to be arrested at once."

All very well, if only Schlummermutz had been there to break up the crowd in the marketplace, to drive the intruders out of the Town Hall and to take Gundula Immofila into custody. None of the councilors thought it wise to raise a hand against her. Not only because the blacksmith with his hammer and several other stalwart workmen with their tools stood behind her—but because the bees had swarmed out of her cap and swirled around her head, buzzing dangerously. Lora sat on her shoulder with feathers puffed and eyes sparkling fiercely, and Minette was scratching her claws on the floor-length velvet cloth of the conference table.

Up to this moment the mayor had not noticed Trippstrill and Winkelriss. When he did, he gasped for breath and his yellow eyes blinked like the eyes of an owl suddenly confronted with bright daylight.

"Down with tyranny!" Gundula cried. "Our cup is full

to overflowing. We want liberty. Here stand the two honest men whom you put behind bars because they were in your way. Who knows better than you that they are innocent?"

"The stone virgin," Winkelriss said. "Nobody believes *we* made away with her."

"Where is she?" Trippstrill demanded. "Confess where you have hidden her!"

Gundula raised her hand and pointed her finger at the golden chain of office across the mayor's chest. "Yes," she said. "You are the one. One of the selfsame pair who menaced our town three hundred years ago. Go back to your coffin, Earl Owl of Owlhall! Back where you belong!"

As though a magic word had been spoken, the frozen row of councilors jerked into motion. Their heads bobbed back and forth, jerked this way and that, as each man sought to see how the others reacted, and their faces contorted in fear. The mayor stood for a moment as if listening, as if he were hearing a command that he had to obey. His face changed with incredible speed. The nose jutted forward and turned down to become the beak of a predatory bird; wings sprang from his shoulders; his robe changed into puffed-out feathers; his yellow eyes stared murderously, and from the bill came nothing but a hoarse hooting. Quicker than words can tell there suddenly sat a huge owl on the arm of the mayor's chair, and in place of the councilors a flock of crows rose up.

For a moment they all seemed to hurl themselves at Gundula's head. But Lora, Minette and the bees took care of that. The bees boomed threateningly. Lora, sitting on Gundula's shoulder, screamed and beat her wings. Her sharp beak would have been a match even for the big owl. Minette had jumped on the table and stood there spitting, with gleaming eyes, ready to spring on any of the black birds who dared come too near her mistress.

"Easy, easy," Gundula said. "No reason for bloodshed, my dears." She was holding the door of the balcony wide open. "Please, your honor, Earl Owl of Owlhall," she said with perfect politeness. "Please, gentlemen."

The people in the square stared openmouthed when they saw a small, dark cloud rush from the open door, fly up in the pale sky and dissolve into nothing.

And then Gundula Immofila stepped out on the balcony and looked down on her fellow citizens thoughtfully.

The crowd had meanwhile grown even bigger; down in the square all was a swarming and humming as in a beehive when the queen is preparing for her wedding flight.

"Vogelsang is free again!" Gundula announced. "An evil spirit has ruled over our peaceful town and made mischief everywhere. I have called him by his right name and that has finished him. There is no longer anyone threatening your rights. Go home and fry eggs, bake Easter cakes and color all the Easter eggs you please. You will find a plentiful supply in the Town Hall cellar, and they belong to all of you by rights. Tomorrow, on Good Friday, go quietly to church. Day after tomorrow the whole town is invited to a free performance at Pampini's circus, and the marionette theater will also give performances free for grownups and children."

"Hurrah!" the cheers rang up from the square. "Hurray for Gundula Immofila. Long live freedom!"

And at this moment all the birds in their cages began trilling and singing with all their might, and high above the square a jubilant flock of chirping songbirds flew past. For Snow White had gnawed holes in the nets that were to have caught them by droves.

"Hish, hish," Gundula went, and the bees which had settled in the fur of her cap rose into the air, circled about her head for a moment and then flew off toward Cathedral Hill and their hive.

"And now would you mind explaining how all this happened, dear friend!" Winkelriss and Trippstrill urged her. "How did you know what to do, and where is the stone virgin? Where are Lena and Tina?"

"Please ask me no questions now," Gundula said. "Come to my studio after midnight and you'll hear the whole story."

Without waiting for a reply she turned away from them and went down the stairs and out to the square again, where the populace greeted her with joyful cries. The whole throng accompanied her part of the way and then broke up into gay groups which went their separate ways through the narrow alleys of the Old Town. Soon afterwards the pleasant fragrance of frying eggs came wafting from all the houses.

Gundula, however, did not go toward her home on Cathedral Hill. Instead she made briskly for Eusebius's house on Market Street, talking under her breath as she walked as if it were necessary to convince herself. "After all, I can't just let him die of pneumonia all alone, even though he does deserve to a hundred times over. Besides, it will do him good to learn that for once he was mistaken. Limited mental horizon, indeed! Medieval superstition! I'd like to know what he is going to say about today's work, the stuck-up simpleton!"

In this mixed mood of Christian loving-kindness and self-righteousness, she climbed the winding staircase and knocked on the door to Eusebius's bachelor quarters. She waited, then knocked harder. Finally, when there was no answer to her repeated pounding, she opened the un-locked door and stepped into Eusebius's room.

What a mess the place was in! She made a path through scattered papers and stacks of books to the bed. From the wall threatening and horrible masks from South Sea islands grinned at her. Strange weapons seemed to be aimed at her; white sea-shell eyes of wooden fetishes stared severely.

There was nothing of Eastertide peacefulness in her mood as she hewed her way toward the bed. "Nonsense," she said severely. "Nonsense and fiddlesticks. Just an-other one of your silly tricks, pretending you are dying from a simple cold." But the bedclothes stayed so strangely still that all at once her heart contracted with dread. And when she stepped closer and thrust back the quilt, as if she expected to find Eusebius crouching under the blan-kets to play a joke on her, she saw to her nameless horror that the bed was empty.

"Too late!" she breathed, and covered her eyes with the palm of her hand.

Meanwhile Anemone had resigned herself. She had decided to be a good girl and obey Aunt Gundula's order not to leave the house. Maybe this wasn't tyranny after all. Maybe Gundula had strong reasons to keep her safely at home. But even grownups cannot always carry out their good intentions.

Outside the wind was still howling and whistling through the streets. Now and then it made a loose plank on one of the booths in Cathedral Square flap back and forth. It twirled hats off the heads of men and whipped women's petticoats over their heads. For a while Ane-mone had great fun watching all this from the window. But soon after Aunt Gundula had gone it looked as though

the same wind were blowing all the people away from
Cathedral Square and down narrow Market Street. So
the scene from the window became pretty dull. If only
Winnie and Lora, Minette and Snow White had been
here Anemone would not have found the time hanging
so heavily on her hands. But as it was, she did not feel
like reading any more today, and her aunts were no en-
tertainment either. They sat in moody, mournful silence
and paid no attention to her. And so Anemone wandered
about the studio, bored and cross, and finally stood lost
in thought in front of the egg with the pretty girl and the
chocolate lad who looked exactly like Uncle Eusebius,
only younger and handsomer.

If he hadn't died of pneumonia yet, something—absolutely—ought to be done for him. As usual these
grownups never gave a thought to the most obvious things.
Certainly if a man were very sick and there was one last
little thing which would give him pleasure, that thing
should be done. Anyone in his right mind could see that.
And this beautiful egg with a portrait of Eusebius on it
seemed to Anemone the perfect gift. He could not help
perking up a bit when he saw it; after all, it showed that
Aunt Gundula at the bottom of her heart really wasn't
so awfully mad at him.

The more Anemone considered the matter, the more
sensible it seemed to her. And once she took a notion
into her head, she usually carried it out. With the reassuring feeling that this was the only right thing to do,
she seized the egg and sneaked out of the room. Her two
aunts did not so much as glance her way.

As she climbed the steps to Eusebius's flat, she could
hear him sneezing and snuffling just like the dragon in
the marionette show. The sounds were rather comforting,
for then he was still alive. But what a state the poor man

was in. All alone and neglected, he lay in a tumbled bed, nose and face red and swollen. Anemone's eyes filled with tears of pity at the spectacle before her. No one had puffed up the pillows for him, no one had laid a cold compress on his hot forehead, or a hot-water bottle on his cold feet. He did not even have anything hot to drink. The stove had gone out and stood cold and black in the disordered room.

"This just won't do!" said the feminine little creature in Perdu's boy's clothing. And she energetically made a stab at setting the room to rights.

"Whoever you are," a hoarse voice, interrupted by frequent sneezes, croaked from the bed, "what a mercy that someone has come to see me at last. It serves me right, though—this is what happens to a man who prefers to go on a trip around the world rather than marry a wonderful girl. Now there's no one to care for me and I shall die alone and abandoned."

"Maybe you won't have to die yet," Anemone consoled him. She tried in vain to start a fire in the cold stove. "No, it won't catch. That's the last match in the box and there's no kindling either. You can't stay here with the stove out. By the way, you may as well call me Anemone, only don't tell anyone."

In his delirium poor Eusebius had been dreaming so many wildly improbable things that the appearance of Anemone in boy's clothing and with cropped hair did not even surprise him. "Anemone?" he gasped feebly. "Oh, if it really is you I can only say thank God!"

"I'll take care of you," Anemone assured him. "You're just coming along with me. There's so much room in Aunt Gundula's four-poster that we can easily fit you into it, too. Come, get your clothes on, it's just a few steps across the square."

"Hold on, now!" Eusebius cried out. "You don't know what you're saying. To Gundula's? Not for all the world. Do you think a woman of her caliber would ever forgive me for the way I've behaved?"

"That doesn't matter at all now. Of course you have been rather silly. How could you send that article to the newspaper about limited horizons and so on? Your trip was bad for you. People shouldn't stay away so long. But look at this. Do you think that anyone who paints such a beautiful Easter egg for a person is so mad at him that she'll never forgive him? Well?"

And under Eusebius's sore and flaming nose she held the wonderful egg. He reached for it with both hands, examined it from all sides, gazed at it again and again, beside himself with amazement and emotion. "Has she sent me this, Anemone? Did she tell you to bring it to me?"

"Well, she didn't exactly tell me to," Anemone admitted. "You can ask her yourself later. But now the main thing is to move you into a warm room and a fresh bed."

Eusebius was too sick and too bemused by the sight of that beautiful egg and the word UNFORGOTTEN to put up any real resistance. Obedient as a lamb he let Anemone wrap him in his coat and swaddle his neck in a woolen muffler which she had picked out of the clutter of the room. She pushed a fur cap far down over his head, put on his rubbers and led him out across Cathedral Square and up the many steps to Aunt Gundula's apartment. In his numbed mind he only felt a dim gratitude; it was so pleasant to submit to the guidance of someone who knew just exactly what she wanted. He supposed everything else would turn out all right. There was a beautiful peace and sense of security in putting himself completely in Anemone's hands.

A door from the hallway led into the bedroom, and so it was not difficult to smuggle Eusebius in unnoticed by Aunts Lena and Tina. Anemone helped him into the Dream Ship and covered him up to the tip of his nose. His poor thrumming head sank into the soft pillow. Ah, how long it was since he had lain in such a clean, white and fragrant bed. Before he knew what was happening or had a chance to ask a question, he fell fast asleep. Anemone stole out of the room on tiptoe. In the studio she picked up another volume of Shakespeare.

She was altogether lost in *The Tempest* and thinking of nothing else when the door flew open and in came Aunt Gundula like a whirlwind, followed by Minette, Snow White, Lora and Winnie. Anemone jumped up and, not even greeting her aunt in her impatient affection, threw her arms around Winnie.

But what a sight the poor dog was. Nothing was left of her fancy paint or the sugar-coating on her beard. Wind and rain, the underbrush in the woods and the juniper in the pastures had scraped and scratched her fine coat. It was a wet, filthy, and bedraggled little dog that sank down at her mistress's feet.

"You, too, will wear a star on your collar like your great ancestor Skilligaly, Winnie," Aunt Gundula said. "The Double Star of Vogelsang. Without you and Blue Boy, without Minette, Lora and Snow White, and good Kim and my brave bees we would never have won the great Easter Egg Battle. But now change Winnie back into a Kerry, Anemone, and yourself into a girl. The time for masquerades is past."

Aunts Lena and Tina overwhelmed Aunt Gundula with questions. While she was giving them a brief account of what had happened, Anemone fetched a tub of warm water and a sponge and soap. She washed the mud and

the remains of the paint off Winnie and wrapped the dog
in a soft towel. Thus swathed, Winnie settled down in
the basket beside Minette and Snow White, while Lora
flew up on her pole. "You had better stock up on sleep,"
Aunt Gundula said to the parrot. "There will be more
work for you to do tonight."

Everyone looked questioningly at her, but Aunt Gundula did not choose to explain. "It's all over," she said.
"The Wicked Owl is dead, let's hope for good this time.
Your husbands are free—I've asked them to come here
at midnight. Now the task remains to make the stone
maiden return to her niche. But I think we will manage
that too."

At the news that their husbands were alive and free,
Lena and Tina threw their arms around Gundula. And
Anemone pricked up her ears as she listened. She thought
how wonderful it would have been if *she* had been riding
Kim's back instead of Ajunta, when the elephant battered
down the doors to the Town Hall. But she sat quiet as a
mouse because she did not exactly look forward to giving
an account of *her* day.

Aunt Gundula's eyes were moving uncertainly about
the room. "Well, light the candles," she said in an oddly
choked voice. "Oh, who would ever have thought they
would be funeral candles! Eusebius is no longer among
the living. They've taken him away already. . . ." Her
voice broke. She looked once more at the candles which
Anemone had obediently gone and put a match to, albeit
with a sinking feeling that the time for explanations had
come. "Help!" Aunt Gundula suddenly cried out. "The
egg is gone!"

There was a minute of embarrassed silence. Distressed
and wondering, Lena and Tina looked at one another and
then at Anemone. At last Anemone said in a small voice:

"Pardon . . . I took it to Uncle Eusebius." You never knew how grownups would take something like that, even when you had acted with the noblest intentions. Sometimes good deeds had an effect which was just the opposite of what you might suppose. "I thought, because he's so sick and might be dying and because he looks so much like the chocolate boy and because . . . and because . . ."

"Come to my arms, my good child!" Aunt Gundula sobbed, proving once more that you could never guess how grownups were going to take things. "You gave the poor man a pleasure, one last pleasure, for now he is dead."

"Not quite dead yet, Aunt Gundula," Anemone said, stroking her aunt's tearstained cheek. "He's lying in your bed in the next room sleeping."

Spring Full Moon

No NEWS OF the uprising in the heart of town had as yet reached the house of Benjamin Florus outside St. John's Gate. Erwin had come home late in the evening, tired out and even grumpier than he usually was. He told his mother that they had failed to catch the piebald dog, and that the boy who sold Easter eggs had not turned up all day. He and his gang had chased the dog out into the meadows beyond St. John's Gate. They had scrambled through ditches and run up forsaken roads, leaped fences and plodded over plowed fields and muddy byways, always just behind that unbelievably agile dog until at last they'd given up the chase, and Erwin returned home across the countryside without going back into town.

"It's all right, my darling sweet," Ilsebill consoled him. "I know I can put Mr. Florus in the right mood tonight, and then we needn't worry about Anemone or that ugly dog any more. Just guess what I found in the

wintergarden among the primroses today? Our lovely
herb! I took two leaves right away and made a brew of
them. Once he has drunk that he will forget his child and
dog and his late wife too, if he hasn't already forgotten
them. Then we will be in charge of things here, and if
Anemone doesn't turn up again, so much the better for
us. But if she does ever come back, we'll give her something to think about. Now wash up and comb your hair
nicely and act your best tonight."

She set the table with a white damask cloth and the
finest glasses and china from Mrs. Florus's cupboards.
Then she went to her room to primp a little.

"Today you must forget all your troubles, my dear
Mr. Florus," she said in her cooingest voice when they
were seated at table. "After all, it is the night of the
spring moon. We ought to celebrate that, you know."

"No reason to celebrate," Mr. Florus replied gloomily,
"when I don't know where my child is or what has happened to her."

"Oh, please don't go over that sad business again,"
Ilsebill said. "After all, there was that announcement in
the newspaper saying distinctly that your child is alive
and well. She is just playing hide-and-seek with us, the
cunning little thing. Or perhaps she is sulking because I
had to punish her, although I assure you doing so hurts
me far more than it does her. But you will see, by Easter
Sunday the dear child will be back. I feel it in my bones.
I just know she will be."

"And then won't I give it to her!" Erwin growled
between his teeth, and received a look of indulgent re-
proof from his mother.

"My Erwin spent his whole day again looking for
Anemone and Winnie," Ilsebill went on. "He couldn't
possibly enjoy Easter without his two playmates. He's

such a good child, simply doesn't have it in him to hold a grudge, even though Anemone and Winnie have been mean to him at times."

She began serving the meal, and again there was one of Mr. Florus's favorite dishes, mushroom patties with herb sauce and sponge dumplings. Though he had hardly any appetite, Mr. Florus could not help praising the delicious meal. The table setting was attractive and festive; wine sparkled in the crystal glasses; the salad was a sight to behold. But there was something lacking, and suddenly Mr. Florus realized that this something had been lacking ever since Ilsebill had begun keeping house for him. Flowers. Queer that she never places flowers on the table, he thought. (Of course he had no way of knowing that flowers withered as soon as Ilsebill's hand touched them.) A table without flowers in a gardener's home! he thought, and his returning good temper temporarily clouded over again.

But after all, the door to the wintergarden was standing open, and there was greenery and blossom to your heart's desire. There stood two large palms in their big wooden tubs, as well as scores of camelias and azaleas just opening their pink and coral buds, while row upon row of pots of flowering primroses carpeted the floor.

"I really am grateful to you for all the trouble you go to, my dear Ilsebill," Mr. Florus said, trying to look a bit friendlier. "You take such good care of my home and go to such efforts for my sake, although I am afraid I am dull company for you these days."

"Oh," Ilsebill whispered, bowing her head demurely over her plate. "What would I not give to be able to banish your grief and make you gay and cheerful again."

Then she changed the plates and brought up the heavy artillery, with which she was planning to breach the for-

tress: a huge platter of golden cream puffs, bursting with
snow-white whipped cream.

Mr. Florus sighed deeply, and his resistance gave out.
As he devoured the first cream puff he reflected that he
was unusually lucky to have found such a capable housekeeper and good cook as Ilsebill. With the second cream
puff it occurred to him that he ought to try to make sure
he did not lose her. The third and fourth cream puffs
brought to mind the thought that in addition to her do-
mestic talents she seemed to be distinctly fond of him.
Besides which, the green dress she was wearing tonight
was very becoming indeed. And as he started on the fifth
cream puff it flashed through Mr. Florus's head: I ought
to marry her! Really, that was the thing to do.

Now she filled his glass with a dark dessert wine,
handed it to him and said in honeyed tones: "Let us drink
to a continued happy life together. Alas, sometimes dark
forebodings come to me that a cruel fate may drive me
away from this good house which has been like a home
to me and my fatherless boy. Indeed, I know I do not
deserve the good fortune of spending my life serving so
wonderful a person as yourself."

She spoke these words with a faint quaver in her voice,
and dabbed her handkerchief at her eyes, although they
were as dry as the desert sands. Then, with a wistful
smile, she lifted her glass to touch it to his. But she
instantly set it down again, for Erwin had leaped to his
feet shouting, "A mouse, a white mouse!" and rushed
out into the wintergarden.

"Oh dear!" Ilsebill sighed, pressing her hand to her
heart. "What is that? I think I am going to faint."

Mr. Florus jumped up and bent in alarm over the
woman, who was slowly collapsing into her chair. But
then, from the top of one of the potted palms in the
wintergarden, came a croaking voice:

"Mr. Florus, now beware,
Venom here and poison there!
Let the magic wine alone.
Hearts of stone are only stone.
At the full of Easter's moon
Things will disentangle soon.
Anemone again your own,
Heart to heart and stone to stone."

"What does this mean?" Mr. Florus asked in astonishment, rubbing his forehead as though trying to shake off a nightmare.

"Witchcraft!" Ilsebill cried out, in so loud a voice that there seemed no longer to be any question of her fainting. She threw her arms around Mr. Florus's neck. "Deviltry and witchcraft! They're trying to rob you of your happiness and make me homeless again. You're upset, dear Mr. Florus—have a sip, that will calm you."

But Mr. Florus uneasily pushed the glass aside, and once more the voice from the palm tree recited:

"Let the magic wine alone.
Hearts of stone are only stone."

"Don't listen, don't listen to the nonsense!" Ilsebill implored him. And from the wintergarden came Erwin's voice: "It bit me, the nasty beast bit me. And it's gone and gnawed off our little herb. Mama, look, it's carrying it away."

"Catch it!" Ilsebill screamed, beside herself. "Catch it and save the herb!"

At this there was a fluttering among the leaves of the palm, and with a flash of emerald wings a parrot flew into the room. It settled on the table and with its beak knocked over Mr. Florus's glass. The dark wine poured like blood over the white tablecloth.

"Lora!" Mr. Florus exclaimed, and the bird rubbed its head like an old friend against his hand. "Why, this is Gundula's Lora!"

But at the spilling of the wine Ilsebill lost all control of herself. "You miserable bird!" she screamed. "Wait till the Wicked Owl catches you!" She seized a knife lying on the table and rushed like a fury at the bird. Head tilted to one side, Lora eyed her calmly.

God help us! Mr. Florus thought as he saw his housekeeper's face contorted with rage. He tugged at his collar as though he were finding it hard to breathe. "Let Lora alone," he said with a sharpness he had never used before toward Ilsebill. But Lora could take care of herself. A lift of her wing and she had flown from the table to the cupboard, and thence to the curtain pole, still croaking her verse:

> "*Anemone again your own,*
> *Heart to heart and stone to stone.*"

Meanwhile Erwin, chasing the mouse, had left the farther door of the wintergarden open to the street. Lora saw her chance to escape and flew into the garden. Ilsebill, out of her senses with rage and hatred, followed her into the moonlit night.

Mr. Florus did not call her back. With a sense of relief he would not have been able to explain, he quietly closed the door after her.

Outside, Lora flew from bush to bush, from fence post to fence post, with Ilsebill always just behind her. Sometimes the woman came so near that it seemed she would be able to plunge her knife into the bird's heart the very next moment. Now Lora flew up to the top of

St. John's Gate; now she hopped along the street as though she had injured a wing and could no longer fly. Once she made a halt on the pavement and let Ilsebill come almost up to her, only to take flight again at the last moment.

"The herb!" Ilsebill cried after Erwin. "You must get the herb away from that mouse!"

The moon stood high and bright over the deserted street. Black clouds mantled it now and then, but they would pass and its silvery light would break through. Now and then a gust of wind lashed savagely out of a side street and tugged at the woman's dress as she single-mindedly followed the bird, the mouse and Erwin. When they reached Cathedral Square, the strange little procession, in a series of erratic dashes, made its way up the steps of the cathedral. The wind attacked them up there with renewed fury. Lora let Ilsebill come closer and closer to her. The white mouse darted hither and thither, the slip of green herb twitching in its mouth like a victory trophy. Now the nimble little creature was climbing up the stone wall of the cathedral and Erwin scrambled after it with monkeylike agility. Lora fluttered into an empty niche and dropped down, apparently utterly exhausted. Fired by her rage, Ilsebill put her foot on a jutting bit of carving in the wall, pulled herself up, and clambered up the buttress. She stretched out her hand with the knife. "Now I have you!" she panted with the little breath she had left.

Once more the bird croaked: "Heart to heart and stone to stone," and high above from the cathedral tower the first strokes of midnight rang out. Good Friday had begun.

"The herb, Erwin, the herb," Ilsebill muttered. Faint with exhaustion, she leaned against the back of the niche.

But Erwin did not reply. The mouse scurried away, the bird took flight. When the twelve strokes had solemnly faded away, there was no longer an empty niche on the west wall of the cathedral. All the Virgins, Wise and Foolish, were standing as they had always stood in their places, and above one of them hung the repulsive waterspout, lips pursed. On the stones below an insignificant sprig of green weed lay withering.

Meanwhile, Anemone's three aunts, eagerly assisted by Anemone herself, had been lavishing attentions upon poor Eusebius. They let him sleep for a while. Then Aunt Gundula went over to the big bed and, without condescending to converse with the patient, began heaping blanket upon blanket and featherbed upon featherbed over him, until only Eusebius's nose showed sharp and red from under the mountain of whiteness. Meanwhile Anemone had heated water in the kitchen. Aunt Tina filled hot-water bottles and mason jars and thrust them under the covers. Aunt Lena had brewed some lilac tea, and now held a cup of this concoction to his lips although he croaked in desperate protest: "Grog! Grog would be better for me! My weak heart can't stand lilac tea."

"Weak heart, eh," Aunt Gundula said mildly, as though speaking to a fussy child. "Exactly! His heart has always been the weakest part of his anatomy."

They made him sweat profusely. Every few minutes one of the nurses went over and wiped his burning face with a cool sponge. Nor did they fail to place cold compresses on his forehead.

"I'm melting away," Eusebius wailed in a dying voice, and in his black ingratitude he even thought he had been better off in his bachelor room without female attendance. "Mercy!" he pleaded. "It's enough. I'm well again."

But such ravings went as good as unheard. With lenient smiles the women tucked the blankets in even tighter at the sides of the bed. "You have to sweat it out of you," they said. "That's the only effective treatment against a cold." They let him swelter until they decided his body had been thoroughly cleansed of all sickness—and perhaps also of the poison of the ideas he had picked up on his trip around the world.

But his trials were not yet over. For now the mountain of blankets was removed and poor steaming Uncle Eusebius was sponged with cold water so long and so violently that he feared his skin was being stripped off. Then they rubbed him down with soft towels and sat him up, wrapped again in blankets, in a chair. Meanwhile the bed was remade with fresh linen and he was handed one of Aunt Gundula's nightgowns, fragrant with lavender. The three aunts, and Anemone also, bustled about with the greatest energy and rivaled one another in their efforts to make the sick man as comfortable as possible now. Finally Aunt Gundula fixed him a drink of honey and mixed herbs, a gentle cough-syrup and sleeping draught combined, which Eusebius this time drank without objection. Then he sank back into the pillows, and the happy smile on his face suggested that he was glad to have at last escaped the zealous attentions of his nurses.

A little later, when he raised his heavy eyelids once more and glanced around him, still dazed with sleep, he thought he was in paradise. So I've died after all, he said to himself, his mind pleasantly numbed.

Around him seaweed rippled gently; amid forests of coral swam glittering fish and mother-of-pearl snails. Above him stretched a flowery meadow with innumerable animals living together in peace without preying upon one another. Magnificent trees, some of them still flowering, the others already laden with fruit, towered into the delicate blue of the sky, and in and among their branches bright-colored birds perched and fluttered. In the distance a snow-crowned chain of mountains glittered blue-white, and high above, where the firmament darkened, stars moved in their courses in eternal splendor. Somewhere at the summit of it all there was a deep humming as vibrant as the tone of a big bell. The women were flitting about the bedroom like kindly spirits, putting last minute touches to this and that. A little later they betook themselves to the studio and left Eusebius alone. For the second time that evening he sank into a deep sleep and slept the whole night through without a single cough or sneeze.

"Well now," Aunt Gundula said, after they had finished a hearty and well-earned supper. "Go to sleep, Anemone. There's plenty of room for a small person like you in my armchair by the window. You've installed an occupant in my bed, and I shall have to find a place to stay myself. Aunts Lena and Tina will move to other quarters, if I'm not mistaken. Tomorrow we'll decide what you are going to do with yourself from this point on."

"I have already decided," Anemone said. "We're going away with the circus, aren't we, Winnie?"

"Why, child," Aunts Lena and Tina exclaimed, clapping their hands together. "What about your poor father? He'll grieve himself into his grave."

Aunt Gundula looked around at each of them in turn. "A poor lot we are, my dears. It seems to me that of late each of us has thought much too much about herself. Yes, you too, Anemone. It's this way: the offenses others commit against us we carry in a little basket in front of us, so that we always have them handy to look at. But the offenses and unkindnesses and all the hundred little neglects we commit against others every day—these we carry in a big bundle on our backs, so we can't see them. Come, Anemone, sit down now and write a little note to your papa for Easter, so that he'll see you are thinking of him. There's plenty of time still for you to consider about the circus."

"Well, if you think so," Anemone said. She cleared off a corner of the studio table, sat down and wrote in her finest handwriting:

"Dear Papa, I am thinking of you and you need not worry about me because that isn't necessary because I am going to the circus and will be an equestrian which is a super profession and Winnie too. I must tell you that Erwin started that about the darning needle, Winnie and I were almost absolutely innocent, and that's the honest truth, and if you keep him instead of me you'll soon find out what a nasty thing he is. I've been through an awful lot and it's been wonderful only that my aunts go up in the air when I take a little tumble into the vault or something, even though it was so useful because otherwise how could Aunt Gundula have found out that the Wicked Owl's coffin was empty, and his proper name and all. Happy Easter, dear Papa, when I'm famous I'll come to see you sometime. Fondest love from your loving daughter Anemone.

P.S. When *they* are gone, I mean.

P.S.S. Maybe you'll join the circus with me?"

"There," Anemone said, and she wiped off her inky fingers on the blotter.

A bed was made for her on the chair by the window.

Anemone immensely liked the idea of sleeping on a chair for once. She was always in favor of breaks in routine, and there was certainly no lack of these at Aunt Gundula's.

"Do you think he'll get better?" she asked, already half asleep.

"Let us hope so," all three aunts answered in chorus.

When the cathedral clock struck twelve, Gundula went to the window, saying: "Lora and Snow White ought to be home soon."

It was now perfectly quiet outside. The wind had died down; round and unblemished the spring full moon was riding in the dark sky. No owls hooted from the cathedral towers.

"Good Friday," Lena said. "What a Holy Week!"

A sharp beak pecked at the window-pane. On the sill sat Lora, with her claws carefully curled around Snow White.

"There they are!" Gundula cried, opening the window. "And my left elbow is twitching almost unbearably."

At the same moment the doorbell out on the landing rang. Tina hurried out; there was a cry of joy, and she flew into her Agamemnon's arms.

With altogether unwonted haste, Trippstrill rushed into the room and embraced his wife Lena. "She's back!" he cried excitedly. "The Foolish Virgin is standing in her niche again. What do you think of that, my dear? Just as we came up the cathedral steps we saw it, both of us, didn't we, Agamemnon?"

"We surely did," Winkelriss agreed. "My Heavens, what we have gone through on account of that frightful person. It seems like a long bad dream. But now, dear Gundula, please explain."

"Wait just a little longer," Gundula said. "My elbow is still twitching."

She went into the kitchen, and soon a huge bowl of her famous mulled punch stood steaming on the table. Beside it she placed a plateful of Easter cake, and Winnie, Snow White, Lora and Minette were plied with goodies, heaped with praise and showered with caresses. All four were so tired after their strenuous day that they could scarcely enjoy the delicacies that were thrust at them from all sides, and the dog, the cat, and the mouse soon curled up in their basket. Lora did not fly up to the curtain pole tonight. Instead she chose to sleep on the high back of Gundula's armchair, in which Anemone slept so soundly that she noticed nothing of the visitors or the lively conversation among the grownups.

The reunited couples sat hand in hand, looking at one another with radiant eyes as if they could not understand how they had ever been able to part.

"Bewitched," Lena said, shaking her head. "That's what we all have been. As though the henbane had poisoned and blinded us."

Trippstrill nodded agreement, and Winkelriss put his arm around Tina and said, "The main thing is we have each other again. I still cannot fully grasp it. No trial hanging over us, the mayor out of the way, and the Virgin back in her place, as well as that gem of a waterspout. Just as if the whole thing had been a simple nightmare. Truly, a night of wonders."

"Spring full moon!" Gundula said significantly. As she spoke she was thinking half sadly, half gladly: now I shall soon be alone again, the birds of passage will come and I will go back to my work in peace.

The bell rang once more. Winnie, who had been sound asleep, suddenly jumped up, barking joyfully, and rushed to the door. In stepped Mr. Florus, to be heartily greeted by his friends.

"Where is she?" he called. "Where is Anemone? I

couldn't stand it longer alone at home." He ran his hand over his head, finding that he had rushed away without even putting a hat on. "What are you all doing here? They tell me you were in jail, Winkelriss and Trippstrill."

"We were," Winkelriss said. "Haven't you heard all that's been happening? The Wicked Owl who has been bullying us is back in his tomb, the jinx of a statue back in her niche, and we back with our wives."

"The Wicked Owl?" Mr. Florus stammered.

"About that later," Gundula said. "First tell us what's been going on over your way this strange day."

"Strange indeed," Mr. Florus agreed, wiping the perspiration from his forehead and refusing the pastries Gundula was offering him. Those cream puffs still lay like lead in his stomach. "Well, when we were having supper and my housekeeper urged me to drink some wine, your Lora suddenly flew into my house and croaked a couple of peculiar verses. A white mouse was there, too, and my housekeeper took off down the street, she chasing the bird and little Erwin the mouse. Do you really mean to say, that she was the . . . well, yes, I *did* see the missing Virgin standing in her niche at the cathedral again as I passed just now, and I'll choke down another cream puff if she didn't bat her eyes at me."

"That must have been your imagination," Winkelriss said. "She's batted her last eyelash."

"But what about Anemone?" Florus went on. "Don't torment me any longer. I've had all I can stand. Lora promised I would find her."

"Patience!" Gundula said and handed Anemone's letter across the table to him. He read it, but still seemed not to be reassured and looked imploringly at Gundula. She laid a finger on her lips and, leading him by the hand, tiptoed over to the armchair where the girl was sleeping sweetly, her short hair in tousled curls over her bruised forehead, looking for all the world like a rosy, snub-nosed cherub.

"How could she!" Mr. Florus whispered. "How could she run away like that!"

"When you see a needle sticking in someone's earlobe," Gundula replied, "first ask *why* it's sticking there, before you punish somebody. There seem to have been quite a few changes for the worse in your household since that Foolish Virgin and her changeling moved in on you."

"Please don't rub it in, dear friend! It gives me goose-pimples to think what would have become of me and Anemone if you had not sent Lora to me at the very last minute. Let me take her . . ."

"No!" Gundula said firmly. "You cannot take her back tonight. I need her until Holy Saturday. She's become quite a help in Easter egg painting. And then, my friend, I have an excellent recipe for dumplings. I might as well teach her as long as she is here. Besides, it won't hurt her to sleep in a chair for two nights as a penalty. She went out today when I had strictly ordered her to stay home, and on top of it she dumped a cuckoo's egg into my nest. I mean smuggled your worthy friend Eusebius into my Dream Ship."

"Eusebius!" Benjamin Florus exclaimed in wonder. Things were getting more muddled every minute. Besides, his mind was only half on what Gundula was saying; he could not tear his eyes away from his daughter.

But the news of Eusebius struck home with Winkelriss and Trippstrill. "Eusebius?" they repeated. "We looked in on him at his flat, and when we found the place empty we feared the worst. Is he alive? Is he better?"

"He's alive," Gundula informed them. "People don't generally die of a cold."

"What good sense the child had to bring him here!"

Winkelriss said with deep conviction.

"Think so?" Gundula snapped, and she hustled back to the kitchen because the punch bowl needed refilling.

Returning to the studio she was asked to start at the beginning and tell the whole story of the mysterious events of the past week. No one was particularly surprised once all the tangled threads were straightened out; the only mystery was how blind they all had been. They looked at one another and nodded. Yes, of course, the Foolish Virgin had come to life, and the Wicked Owl had risen from his grave. Everything was as clear as day now and in good Vogelsang tradition. Amazed, the men gazed into the smiling, knowing faces of the women.

"Sometimes it might be kind of helpful not to have a logical mind," Gundula said with a modesty which was not altogether without malice.

The men were quick to agree. They gave praise where praise was due: to Tina for having warned them early in the game not to remove the cathedral statues from their places. To clever Lena for remembering the old chronicles. To Anemone, whose inquisitive little nose had ferreted out such a lot of invaluable information. To Winnie who had been the chief breadearner of the three-aunt household. And to Minette-the-Cat, Lora and Snow White for their fine co-operation. But above all Gundula was praised for using her wonderful insight—and maybe a little witchcraft, too, to make everything turn out well in the end.

"After Anemone had discovered the empty tomb there was nothing to it," Gundula said. "Nevertheless, I couldn't resist the temptation to check up on the whole matter myself. Early this morning I sneaked out and tried to slip through the crack between Moses and Jeremiah to get down into the forgotten vault. But the famous camel may more easily go through the eye of the needle than a grown person squeeze through the narrow margin between legend and life."

"In other words you were a little too plump to get through, weren't you, Gundula dear?" Tina asked—she who was so often teased about her own plumpness.

"There *was* no crack," Gundula said, "any more than there is an indication of my being plump."

The others nodded thoughtfully. But Gundula was not yet finished. "Spooky stories," she went on, "that is what our good fellow citizens will say, and will boast about the fact that things happen in Vogelsang which simply don't happen in other towns. But what do we human beings in our blindness mean by spookiness? What do we know about the forces which unleash ghosts, and where does logic begin and end? Maybe we here in Vogelsang are merely closer to elemental powers than other people.

There was a long, thoughtful silence, while the level in the bowl of punch sank lower and lower.

"But now let us hear from you, you mystifying marionetters," Tina said at last. "How much woe you would have spared us if you had told us the truth."

"We had woe enough of our own," Winkelriss declared. "It was frightful. An empty house, nobody to talk to, worrying about you. I couldn't have stood much more of it."

"And weren't we right in warning you?" Lena could not refrain from saying.

"Of course you were both right, as always," Tripstrill said, looking honestly penitent. "But you, too, are not entirely innocent of blame. After all, the touchstone of love is the ability to trust blindly. For weeks we worked day and night writing and planning, carving, painting, pasting, sewing, putting things together. But there was no telling beforehand whether our marionette show would be a success. In order not to disappoint you we had to keep it all a secret for the time being."

"And besides we wanted so much to earn a little Easter surprise for you," Winkelriss added, rather bashfully. "You'll find it at home, Tina. It's the sunshade of lace you admired so much in Fräulein Putzig's millinery shop."

"Oh, Aggy, how extravagant!" Tina exclaimed, blushing with joy.

"And for you, Lena," Trippstrill said, "I have the little Florentine hat with the bunch of violets—remember, the one you have been looking at in Fräulein Putzig's window ever since Christmas!"

Lena was so moved that she could not say a word. She was very easily moved, and then her eyes always began to water which embarrassed her a good deal. She used to say that it was a kind of nose trouble that made them so watery.

Suddenly from the depths of the chair by the window seat a sleepy voice asked: "And Aunt Gundula? What does she get? Shouldn't she have the blood red ruby . . ."

Gundula signaled to Mr. Florus to remain still and stepped over to Anemone's chair. With raised finger she said sternly, "When I was a child, young folks were not allowed to ask pert questions at one o'clock in the morning."

"It can't be so late," Anemone murmured, looking up at Aunt Gundula with an expression of almost angelic innocence. "Please stop being mad at me because I disobeyed just one single time. I felt so awfully, awfully sorry for him."

"Just one single time!" Gundula sighed. "I think my gray hairs have doubled in this one week."

She looked down at Anemone who had cuddled in her pillows again and instantly gone back to sleep. On her forehead there was a green and blue bruise; her elbows were skinned and her right knee cut and brown with iodine. The blanket had slipped down, and Gundula put it back again over the sleeper. "The little imp!" she said softly to herself. "I'll miss her. Oh, I'll miss her terribly."

All's Well That Ends Well

THERE WAS STILL a great deal to do in the two days
before Easter in Aunt Gundula's attic studio. A beautiful
egg had to be painted for each of the friends. Besides
which Eusebius needed constant nursing, though he was
getting better by the minute. Aunt Gundula, expelled
from her own bed, slept on the narrow and rather hard
couch in the studio. On Good Friday night she sat long
at her table, writing busily. Saturday morning Eusebius
was able to get up and join Gundula and Anemone at the
breakfast table. Gundula looked rather pale and sleep-
worn, but she tried to keep up a lively conversation,
which she thought better than to let Anemone start asking
questions. After breakfast she ordered Eusebius back to
bed again, telling him she had started a new chapter of
her bird book last night and putting a fat volume, entitled
History of the Town of Vogelsang, on his blanket.

"Do you good to re-learn what you've forgotten about

141

your home town," she said tartly. Whereupon she vanished with Anemone into the kitchen and stayed there the rest of the morning.

Anemone helped her aunt with the greatest eagerness and diligence. Under Aunt Gundula's directions she was permitted to make the big star-shaped medallions of pastry and marzipan which were the animals' Easter gifts. The medals were covered with chocolate frosting and heavily sprinkled with chopped almonds and raisins. The name of the recipient was marked on each, in sugar icing, and Anemone painted a scroll of honor on fine white paper which stated that the decoration itself might be eaten since it was to be renewed each Easter.

On the eggs for each of the friends Aunt Gundula painted a pretty dove with an olive branch in its beak flying with outspread wings over the skyline of Vogelsang.

Anemone herself was given an egg almost as beautiful as the one she had taken to Eusebius. On it a little dog and a little girl skipped over a flowery meadow. Lora, Minette and Snow White also fitted into the scene, and Anemone was specially pleased to note that the girl on the egg had a fine straight nose without the slightest tip-tilt to it. On the other side of the egg, wreathed by spring flowers, were the words: "Heart to heart and stone to stone."

"Does that mean Ilsebill and Erwin had to turn to stone again because they had no hearts?" Anemone asked.

Aunt Gundula nodded. "It means that only a loving heart can win another."

That started Anemone off on a torrent of questions. Aunt Gundula finally held her ears and begged: "Stop, stop! You can talk a person deaf, dumb and blind. I really don't know whether Ilsebill will make another stab at obtaining a soul for herself three hundred years from now, or whether the Wicked Owl will ever again return to threaten the liberties of Vogelsang. I imagine it will depend on whether the townsfolk of that time are ready to fight for freedom as we were. I can't tell you whether your father would have turned to stone if he had married Ilsebill, adopted the little monster Erwin, and forgotten about his obedient and gentle daughter Anemone. And I also don't know when your beloved Uncle Eusebius will be back on his feet again so that we can risk letting him walk across the drafty square to go back to his own comfortable home. And now will you kindly hurry up, because it's time for us to get dressed and go to the marionette theater and the circus."

The farewell performance of Pampini's circus started at Saturday noon, and it was a tremendous success as Gundula had predicted. The big tent was filled to the last place. The marionette show had to be given three times in succession because the tiny theater could not seat all those who lined up at its door.

At the circus the three ladies, with Anemone, occupied the place of honor in Director Pampini's red velvet box, Yolanda Pampini sitting with them in her gorgeous purple Sunday dress. Anemone, once more in girl's clothing, leaned up against the railing, eagerly watching so that for this last time she should not miss one single feature. She was still carrying her nose a good inch higher than usual today, for sheer conceit in sitting beside so famous a personage as Aunt Gundula. For wherever Gundula Immofila appeared her grateful fellow-citizens cheered her wildly. Besides which, some of the luster of Winnie's success naturally rubbed off on Anemone. Lady Pooh, no longer the Piebald Dog, but dressed in her natural, elegant silver-gray, was once more given a tremendous ovation and showered with chocolate bars, juicy bones and sausages. It was quite an experience for a little dog to take without growing haughty. But Winnie cared nothing for fame and glory; she was content with the love of her mistress and the friendship of Blue Boy.

There were good-byes to say after the performance— and how hard these were.

"Farewell, Kim!" Anemone said, bravely swallowing her tears. Tenderly she stroked the elephant's rough trunk, which Kim alternately wound around her neck or ran caressingly over Winnie's silky little head. "And you, darling Bijou, and you, Rosalie!" Anemone went on. She had brought sugar, apples, and carrots, and each of the animals received his share. All the wonderful horses came up to her and carefully took the lumps of sugar from her outstretched hand, which grew stickier and stickier by the minute. But no one minded when, with those sticky hands, she threw her arms around Signorina Bella, Peeps, Monsieur Renard the Strong Man, Ajunta and Mr. and Mrs. Pampini. "Who would think Perdu una ragazza!" Yolanda Pampini said, shaking her head and kissing Anemone, and her husband clapped his hands and rolled his eyes and shouted: "Una ragazza! A girl! Didn't she fool us! And now we must go on without Perdu and Lady Pooh! And she was our great attraction! She was magnifico! We'll be miserable without the two of you! Completely miserable!"

"I'm afraid I have to keep on with school a little longer," Anemone said. "And Aunt Gundula says Papa would be awfully sad if I don't come back to him. Anyway Ilsebill and Erwin are gone now. But when I'm grown-up I will take that job, Mr. Pampini. That won't be long now. We have two ponies at our nursery garden. I can practice bareback riding on them meanwhile. Oh,

I don't know any place in the whole world besides home and Aunt Gundula's where I'd rather be than here with you and your animals and all you nice circus people."

And then all her swallowing did not help—tears gushed out of her eyes and her nose started sniveling. But since Anemone as usual had no handkerchief, all her good friends came rushing to her aid. Peeps took out his big, red-checked one; Mrs. Pampini alternately wiped her own face and Anemone's with a blue-checked kitchen towel which she generally had about her person! Signorina Bella extended a tiny, lacy wisp of muslin smelling of violets and Director Pampini held out a big, reassuring white handkerchief. Through her sobs and snuffles, Anemone could not help thinking that it was odd how grown-ups were able to keep their handkerchiefs so white all day long. . . . But then her glance fell on Winnie and Blue Boy, who lay together in the sand of the ring, their heads crossed tenderly, infected by the sadness of their human friends.

"Good heavens!" Anemone exclaimed. "What are we going to do with them? We can't be so cruel as to separate them forever." She looked around the circle for help. But before long a thought occurred to her, which cheered her up completely.

"You know what?" she cried. "You must come to Vogelsang every year—there isn't a nicer town in the world anyway. All year long I'll practice new tricks with Winnie. And when the circus has its summer holiday you can send us Blue Boy for a visit, Mr. Pampini. Won't you?"

"Bene! Benissimo!" the director agreed heartily. "We come back, we want to know Vogelsang better, much better. A jolly town," he chuckled. "A little bizarre, but I like that, I like that very much!"

One last embrace and Gundula tore Anemone away.

"Addio! A rivederci!" The Pampinis waved and all the other artists joined in with: "Auf Wiedersehen!" and "See you again!" and "Au revoir!"

"What are we going to do now?" Anemone asked as she, Winnie and Aunt Gundula once more mounted the steps of Cathedral Hill.

"Now you must take the two eggs to our friends the Winkelrisses and Trippstrills, and when you come back we shall go together to the cathedral for the Resurrection Service."

"And then?"

"And then you will take the third egg and call your Winnie to heel and start off for a certain nursery garden near St. John's Gate."

"I suppose so," Anemone said rather timidly.

"Absolutely," Aunt Gundula replied.

Anemone put in some deep thinking while they climbed the winding staircase. When they opened the door of Gundula's flat, it was very quiet except for Uncle Eusebius's peaceful snorting from the bedroom where he was having his afternoon nap.

"Don't you think Papa should at least have let me say something to defend myself?" Anemone asked—this being the conclusion of her long, hard thinking. "I *was* right in going away, wasn't I?"

"Does it really matter so much to be right?" Gundula said. "Don't you think to love is more important than to win?"

Anemone looked up at her, wide-eyed, and for once she did not say a word. Together they looked down upon the twisting streets of their crazy, beloved town with its lanes and squares, the high gables of its ancient houses and the towers of its churches. It lay down there in the gentle gray-blue of the March afternoon, so peaceful, as

if it were a town just like every other town in Germany.
On the roof garden the three hens were cackling, and the
flock of pigeons from the gable of the sexton's house
kept sweeping out over the square to meet the flock from
the cathedral. Already a crowd of people were streaming
up the many steps of Cathedral Hill for the Resurrection
Service, which is held on Holy Saturday evening in Cath-
olic churches all over the world.

Anemone remembered Gundula's words later when
she sat beside her in the twilight of the cathedral nave.
With pounding heart she looked at the quiet flames of
the candles on the high altar and listened to the choir
singing from the vault where the priests had gathered to
bring the body of Christ back to the high altar from its
tomb where it had been lying among flowers and candles
since Good Friday. "Death, where is thy sting?" the choir
sang softly, and then triumphantly, "Hell, where is thy
victory?"

For the first time in her short life Anemone seemed
to grasp a little bit of the meaning of all this. Wasn't it,
somehow, the same as saying that love is more important
than being right? Sometimes a week can teach you more
than a whole year.

Up ahead, in the carved pew near the altar where the
oldest families of the town had their places, she saw her
father, his face bowed over his hands. And all at once
the last bit of wintry ice melted in her heart and she could
think only that she had hurt him more than he had hurt
her, and how much she loved him.

The organ roared through the cathedral, the bells broke
their week-long silence with mighty peals, the *Te Deum*
swelled to the top of the gothic pillars. "Do you hear the
Gloriosa?" Aunt Gundula asked, as Papa had always
asked her. And then the bell sang and rang out again

with its wonderful, low, serious voice, the glorious Gloriosa of Vogelsang, which is without equal all over the country.

Shortly afterwards a girl with a gray dog went down the cathedral steps and made her way out toward St. John's Gate. The pair grew smaller and smaller in the distance. They passed through the medieval city gate and turned in at the old Florus garden, where in the twilight the dainty crocuses dotted the lawn like so many strokes of a paintbrush dipped in purple, in yellow, in white.

And Gundula? When evening came, she lit the candles on her chest of drawers, and between the candles the beautiful egg was once more reposing in its soft nest of moss. Beside it lay something in a little box, something of gold with a small, glowing spot of red.

The candles burned sweet and still, with that fragrance that only pure wax tapers give. Outside on the roof garden a blackbird sat in the topmost twig of the young plum tree and trilled its spring song in the still, mild evening.

Eusebius sat contentedly in the flower-brocaded chair, a blanket over his knees, which someone had put there thoughtfully. On the back of the chair perched Lora, eying him with head askew as though not quite sure what to make of him. Minette was cleaning herself and looking exactly like the kind of cat who would appear in a person's dreams and utter wise sayings. And Snow White spun round and round a few times and then lay down between Minette's paws, forming a picture of perfect friendship.

"I may keep the egg, then, Gundula?" Eusebius asked meekly.

"I usually eat it for my Easter breakfast," Gundula replied. "But if you want to take it with you . . ."

"No, that isn't how I meant it. It will stay here, of

course, on the chest between those beautiful candles. And although I am sorry for you, I'm afraid you'll have to keep me here too."

"Until you start on your next world tour?" Gundula asked.

Eusebius shook his head. "I'm finished with touring the world. Traveling is apt to turn a Vogelsanger's head, maybe. Besides I have a lot of work to do. After all, I must set the bird songs down in notation for your book, and keep an eye on you so that you'll stop writing in bed at night. With a candle, Gundula! Yes, yes, Anemone told me about this deplorable habit."

"That Anemone!"

"A promising child," he said. "Extraordinarily smart, if you ask me. Don't you agree it's high time there was a sensible man around to look after things?"

Gundula did not answer, so after a while he added, "Provided you have no objections."

On the other side of the square little dots of light were already glowing in the windows. More and more of them appeared. From the cathedral boomed the great melody of the Easter bells.

"Peace on earth," Gundula said.